PEACEFUL GUNS

Johnny Smith gets framed for murder. So, after sending for help from his old man back East, he disappears. His pa, meanwhile, hires a pair of drifting cowpunchers, Buck Lawrence and Zeke Henderson, to find him and clear his name. The two cowboys realize things are getting serious when a couple of attempts are made on their lives. Then things get even worse, and there's no way out until the town of Peaceful is made peaceful again.

Books by Ron Pritchett
in the Linford Western Library:

COUGAR CITY

RON PRITCHETT

PEACEFUL GUNS

Complete and Unabridged

LINFORD
Leicester

11-1999

First Published in Great Britain in 1988 by
Robert Hale Limited
London

First Linford Edition
published 1999
by arrangement with
Robert Hale Limited
London

British Library CIP Data

Pritchett, Ron
    Peaceful guns.—Large print ed.—
    Linford western library
    1. Western stories
    2. Large type books
    I. Title
    823.9'14 [F]
    Uniscroft 14.24

    ISBN 0–7089–5542–8

Published by
F. A. Thorpe (Publishing) Ltd.
Anstey, Leicestershire

Set by Words & Graphics Ltd.
Anstey, Leicestershire
Printed and bound in Great Britain by
T. J. International Ltd., Padstow, Cornwall

This book is printed on acid-free paper

1

Johnny Smith rode slowly through the narrow canyon, letting his horse pick its own way along the dried-up bed of the small arroyo which ran along the bottom. He paid no attention to the rocky walls of the canyon, casting long shadows half-way across the floor of the gorge. His thoughts centred mainly on the dinner he was anticipating when he got back to the ranch house.

Suddenly the sharp *crack* of a rifle echoed and re-echoed off the surrounding cliffs and the bullet whistled past him, ploughing a furrow a dozen yards in front of his horse. Whirling in the saddle, his hand flew to the .36 Whitney Navy revolver nestling by his side, his eyes trying to focus on the canyon rim. His view was hampered by the harsh glare of the setting sun, and he saw no-one. Another shot rang out, the spurt of dust nearer this time. Wildly, he searched for cover. There was no rock large enough to shelter him and, in any case, he was not sure from which direction the shots had come.

Then he espied a sandstone buttress over to his right, containing what looked like a small cave. Spurring his horse over to it, he leapt to the ground as another slug bounced off the buttress, showering him with dust. Diving in the cave, he heard two more shots but the expected searing pain as the bullets hit him did not materialise and he was safe, for the moment.

'Damn' lousy shots,' he grunted to himself as he explored his surroundings. The cave was small, dotted with little rocks and stones, and just large enough for him to turn around in. There was no sign of any snakes, for the thought had crossed his mind that this was rattle-snake country.

Edging forward slowly towards the cave mouth, Navy in hand, Johnny bitterly regretted leaving his Henry .44

rimfire lever action back at the bunkhouse. With a rifle he would have stood a chance at this long-range stuff; with only a pistol his target had to be a whole lot nearer.

There was nothing to be seen along the far wall of the canyon. No more firing had taken place after his undignified dive into the cave, but for all he knew his attacker, or attackers, could be just sitting waiting for him to poke his fool head from the cave entrance. And he had every intention that his head should stay where it belonged — on his shoulders.

It was about an hour to sundown and Johnny resolved to wait for the cover of darkness before making a break for it. He lay prone, a little way back from the cave mouth, gun aimed at the opening.

Half an hour passed and then he thought he heard something. It sounded like a scuffling, followed by a barely audible grunt. He tensed himself, cocked the revolver, and waited grimly.

A shadow flashed past the cave

mouth, and there appeared on the ground a fully-grown rattler, dropped from above. The hideous rattle started at once and the snake lunged forward towards him.

Johnny's Navy roared deafeningly in the cave and the rattler reared in its death spasm, its head blasted from the writhing body. His heart beating furiously and his ears numb from the explosion, Johnny spun another chamber and cocked the gun again. All was silent.

As the stillness continued and the shadows lengthened right across the canyon floor his thoughts stopped racing and he began to cogitate. He had been out all day on the PF eastern range, searching the brush, timber and scrubland where a few mavericks might hide themselves. He had found none; that in itself was suspicious, seeing as the PF had had no round-up for at least three years. Since old man Farrow died after the last round-up they had bought little new stock, but there should have been around twenty per cent natural increase each year. None of the other ranchers in the valley had reported any signs of rustling, spreads which were much richer in stock and grassland than the PF. It was not his worry, being only a cowhand, but it was puzzling and he felt sorry for Mrs. Farrow.

His mind went over the day. He had seen no-one on his lone ride, encountered nothing unusual. Until he entered the canyon and the shooting began. Did some unknown rustlers think he had discovered something out there? The shooting itself had been very poor, considering that the ambushers were probably lying in wait and had plenty of time to aim their rifles at a very slow-moving target. Did they want to drive him in the cave, having located it earlier, and then drop the rattler, hoping it would strike and then feign his accidental death? But they must have seen his sixgun and knew he would shoot at anything that moved near the cave entrance.

Johnny shook his head in bewilderment in the darkening cave. In a few more minutes it would be dark enough outside to risk a break. It was certainly too dark for anyone on the canyon rim to see him. He hoped his horse was still around somewhere and had not decided to take off home on its own, or been captured by his attackers.

His immediate concern was whether anyone was lurking around the buttress, ready to plug him as he left the cave. When it was completely dark, he stuck his hat on the end of his 7½" Navy revolver and cautiously poked it out of the cave mouth. Nothing happened. Drawing it back, he rammed the hat on his head and peered out, his eyes already accustomed to the gloom. Seeing nothing alive, except his horse grazing twenty yards away, he wriggled swiftly on to the still warm rock of the canyon floor, leapt to his feet and flattened himself against the buttress. Then he risked a sprint to the horse, bounded into the saddle without touching the stirrups and urged a speedy departure.

★   ★   ★

On arrival at the PF, Johnny led his horse to the stables and rubbed the sweating animal down with a handful of hay. Then he forked some hay into the manger for it and started feeling around in the dark for a sack of oats; he knew the horse must be as hungry as he was. He had just located it when a revolver roared from somewhere out in front of the ranch house, causing the horses to shy and whinny.

Dropping the oats and drawing his Colt, Johnny raced out and round to the front porch. He glimpsed a shadow moving on the far side, made after it, and promptly sprawled full length over something bulky lying in his path. He leapt to his feet just as the door opened and Alice Farrow peered out, lantern in hand. By the light of the lantern he could see that

7

the object was a body.

'What's the racket?' demanded Alice. 'Sounded like a shot.'

'It was, ma'am. A man's been shot,' Johnny informed her. He could see now the body had a bullet hole in the back.

They looked down as Johnny turned the body over.

It was Dan Beardow, ex-*segundo*, trail boss and ramrod with the PF. He was dead.

'Dan!' cried Alice, and went down on her knees to examine him for signs of life. Dan Beardow had been the only one to stay on after her husband Pete had cashed in his chips. He had managed the place on his own until Johnny showed up and took on the job of cowhand.

'Ain't nothin' we can do, ma'am,' said Johnny.

Alice was staring at the Navy, still in his hand.

'No, ma'am,' exclaimed Johnny, horrified. 'It wasn't me — I was out back in

8

the stables when I heard the shot. Here, feel the barrel, it's cold.'

Alice felt the barrel and nodded. 'Let me see,' she asked.

He handed her the gun and she checked it.

'There's one chamber empty,' she said pointedly.

'Sure, I shot a rattler.'

'It looks bad for you, Johnny,' she said grimly.

'I didn't shoot him, I'd no reason to,' protested Johnny.

'I'm inclined to believe you, son. But who else would, with this evidence?'

Johnny bit his lip. The old girl was right. He'd been found a few seconds after the shot, gun in hand, right over the body.

'I'll have to tell the sheriff what I know,' went on Alice.

'Yeah, I guess you will,' agreed Johnny thoughtfully. 'But give me a chance, huh? If I can find out who it was killed Dan, I will. I know, I'll send for Pa. He's got a lot of influence and money, he'll hire the best detectives around.'

'Guess I can't stop you riding off. But be careful — they may have you lined up for the next shot.'

Johnny grinned. 'Somebody already done that, ma'am. I've been holed up in a canyon till dark. That reminds me, can I get my rifle from the bunkhouse, I shore needed it today?'

'Like I said, I can't stop you. Here, you'd better take your revolver, too.' She handed him the gun.

'Thanks, ma'am,' said Johnny, holstering it. 'No doubt the killer is miles away by now. I'd better shift Dan's body from the porch, it's a mite unseemly.'

With Alice guiding him with the lantern, Johnny dragged the body round to the bunkhouse and covered it with a blanket.

'You go get the sheriff in the mornin',' he told Alice. 'It's too dangerous to go out there alone tonight.'

'And it will give you time to get away,'

she said with a trace of irony.

'Yeah,' Johnny grinned ruefully, picking up his rifle.

'Good luck, Johnny,' called Alice as he rode away into the night.

2

The faded lettering on the little wooden sign on the edge of town bore the legend: 'Welcome to Peaceful'.

The smaller of the two men riding by grinned at his companion.

'Peaceful, huh?' he remarked. 'Wonder if it lives up to its name?'

The speaker was lean and tanned, with calculating green eyes and a week's stubble on his chin. He wore a Montana Peak hat, set at a rakish angle, and typical range garb. A single Peacemaker .45 Colt nestled in the tied-down holster at his thigh, Winchester in the boot at the front of his saddle. But Buck Lawrence was not only dwarfed, he looked positively emaciated by comparison with the other man.

Zeke Henderson was as big as they come. Eight feet by four would be an exaggeration, but that was the impression he gave. His outfit was similar, except for a sugar-loaf sombrero. He wore no gun.

'It'll shore make a change,' Zeke answered at length.

'Yeah,' agreed Buck. 'You know, ever since I hitched up with you, trouble seems to follow us around.'

They rode up the main street of the little cow town. Like so many of its ilk, Main Street seemed to be the only thoroughfare. A few shanties, general store, livery stable, hotel, dance hall, sheriff's office and jail, bank, and the inevitable saloon. None of the buildings had ever seen paint since they were built, and they could just make out the sign 'Bald Eagle Saloon'. They dismounted and hitched their horses, batted some of the dust from their clothes with their hats, and entered.

Four men playing poker at a table in the corner looked up, glanced at Buck, stared at Zeke and kept on staring. The giant had that effect wherever he went. The other two people in the saloon also stared. They were the bartender, a sombre-looking individual with a droopy moustache, and a tall, lean puncher who had been talking to him at the bar.

'What'll it be, gents?' the bartender asked when he came out of shock.

'I'll have a rye,' said Buck, 'and my friend'll have a beer.'

'Make it a big one,' added Zeke. 'It's powerful dusty on the trail.'

'Yessir.' The bartender busied himself.

The poker players returned to their game and the man leaning on the bar nodded in friendly fashion.

'Howdy!' he said. 'Jist passin' through or are yuh fixin' to stay awhile?'

'We've been ridin' apiece,' replied Buck. 'Mebbe we'll stay if'n we like it here. We don't reckon on stayin' in one place too long, but we need to earn a few dollars now an' then.'

'Guess my outfit don't need no punchers at the moment, at least not until round-up time. Mebbe the widder at the PF could use some help though. Her foreman done got hisself shot a while back. Funeral was yesterday.'

Buck shook his head. 'We ain't figgerin' on punchin' no cows for a spell, we're kinda fed up with that. We're lookin' for a new career for a while.'

'Here's yore drinks, gents,' said the bartender. 'That'll be four bits.'

'You ready for a drink?' Buck asked the puncher.

'Thanks, stranger, but I'm with the boys over there,' he said, indicating the poker players. 'We're all from the Bar L.'

'Seein' as how there's only five of you an' it's been a while since we hit a town, I'll buy all of you drinks then. You, too, barkeep, if'n yo're imbibin'.'

'Mighty nice of yuh, mister,' said the bartender, his face breaking into a grin. 'Hear that, boys! Drinks is on the stranger.'

The men at the table waved in friendly fashion.

'I'd better introduce myself,' said the lean puncher. 'I'm Duke Summerville, ramrod of the Bar L. Those four are Art Nelson, Chuck Wiseman, Bart Keene, and Slim Robinson.'

Buck nodded all round. 'I'm Buck Lawrence and my sidekick here is Zeke Henderson.'

'And I'm Ed Williamson,' added the bartender, pouring the drinks.

A pounding of hooves, clattering noise, whinnying of horses and shriek of brakes made them all look up.

'What the hell was that?' asked Buck, staring out of the window. 'I can't see nothin' but dust.'

Ed chuckled. 'That'll be the stage from Brent Creek. Comes in twice a week.'

'Is the driver out to break some kinda record?'

'No, he allus drives like that. He'll be here in a minute, jist as soon as he's unloaded his passengers.'

'Uh-uh. You was sayin', Duke, about somebody gettin' shot,' Buck reminded him. 'How'd it happen?'

Duke took a drink of whiskey. 'There

was a shot the other night, some time after sunset, over at the PF. The Widder Farrow came out to find Dan Beardow, the foreman, lyin' on the porch with a hole in his back. A kid who used to work for us, Johnny Smith, he was standin' over the body with a sixgun in his hand. He took off and ain't been seen since.'

'That ain't quite right,' chipped in the bartender as he delivered the drinks. 'Hank Rawlins was in here last night an' he told me Johnny called in at the telegraph office that same night as Dan was killed. *Then* he disappeared.'

Buck paid him. 'What kind of kid was he, when he worked with your outfit, Duke?'

'That's the funny part,' mused Duke. 'He was a nice, friendly youngster, allus willin' an' helpful. A good cowhand, too. Got on well with the boss, an' especially with his daughter. He's not a killer, I'd say.'

'What about the widder? Did she like him?'

'I dunno. We didn't see much of him

when he went to the PF. But at the inquest she put in a good word for the boy. The facts don't look too good for him, though.'

'Nobody saw nothin' else? Nobody prowlin' around at the time?'

'No.'

The door burst open and a little, bow-legged man, his dusty stetson crammed firmly on his head, came in like a small tornado.

'Howdy, Luke,' said the bartender, setting a whiskey down on the bar, 'them Injuns been chasin' yuh again?'

Luke Simms snorted, rushed up to the bar and downed the drink in one swallow.

'That's better,' he grunted. 'Gimme another. Shore is thirsty work, stage drivin'.'

Buck grinned and Ed poured another shot from the bottle.

'Meet Luke Simms, boys,' said Ed. 'Fastest driver west of the Mississippi. Thinks he's still with the Pony Express.'

'Howdy.' Luke gave Zeke the customary stare and took another drink. 'Ain't seen you boys around before, an' I been all over, from Saint Louis to Pueblo, an' Brownsville to Miles City.'

'We been around, too,' said Buck. 'Only I guess we musta crossed trails at diff'rent times.'

'What yuh doin' in Peaceful?' asked Luke. 'Lookin' for jobs?'

'We was sayin' to Duke here, we're lookin' for a change from punchin'. And trail-drivin'. We've done 'em all, up to Abilene, Ellsworth, Dodge, you name it. We've been clear up to Montanny a few times. And Fort Buford.'

'What was you figgerin' on doin', then?'

'Dunno, there must be somethin' better.'

'Ever try drivin' stage?'

Buck grinned. 'Yeah, we tried it once. Back in the old days, when it was kinda rough. There was allus either Injuns or bandits chasin' us, or long, borin' rides where nothin' happened.'

19

'Them's the kinda rides I get now, the long, borin' ones. Ain't nobody took a shot at me in a coon's age.'

'Any interestin' passengers on today's ride, Luke?' asked Ed.

'Naw. Jist one feller on today. Old coot with store-bought suit on, glasses an' all. Says he's come from out East, Philadelphy or Boston, or somewheres.'

'What would a feller like that be doin' in this God-forsaken place?' Duke asked him.

'Lookin' for his son, he said. Name of Smith.'

'Smith?' reflected Duke. 'That's a pretty tall order. There's a packet of 'em around here, around most places I reckon.'

'Wait a minute,' enthused Buck. 'Wasn't that feller you was talkin' about called Smith — Johnny Smith? The one who disappeared after the murder?'

'Yeah,' agreed Duke. 'Be about the right age, too. Gee, this ain't gonna be very nice for his old man when he finds out, is it?'

A pall of silence fell. Duke took out the makings and rolled himself a cigarette. Buck did the same. Zeke plucked an old corncob pipe out of his vest pocket and looked at it disgustedly.

'Plumb wore out,' he announced. 'Guess I'll jist mosey to the store an' get a new one.'

'Yo're allus buyin' them things,' complained Buck. 'Why don'tcha get a decent briar, it'll last yuh a lot longer? Seems like yuh git a new one in every town we hit.'

''Cos they're sweeter, an' I like 'em sweet. They're cheaper than them imported briars, so I gets more for the same money. That answer yore question, Mister Nosey?'

Buck grinned. 'I guess it does, pardner. You jist go ahead an' spend yore money. We can use a new sack of Bull Durham while yo're there.'

Zeke grunted and strode out.

Duke ordered a fresh round of drinks and Luke opened his mouth to resume the conversation when the door burst open again and a large, beefy individual, sporting a bushy black beard and a pair of old Dragoon .44 Colts, swaggered in. He was followed by a couple of shifty-eyed characters of greatly varying physical attributes. One was buck-toothed, lean as a pikestaff, who seemed to have considerable difficulty in keeping up his pants and chaps. The other wobbled with superfluous flesh, distributed mainly around his middle, giving him a definite pear-shape. Both bristled with guns, like perambulating arsenals.

Black-beard glared insolently at Buck, who smiled back pleasantly, and then his eyes swept the rest of the saloon as he strode over to a table in another corner, away from the Bar L punchers. His two companions followed and sat down.

'Gimme a bottle,' he called to the bartender. 'And bring it over.'

'Comin' right up,' replied Ed, grabbing a whiskey bottle as he came round the bar.

'Who's the polite gent?' asked Buck, keeping his eyes on the trio.

'That's Bull Bartram, foreman at the BE,' replied Duke, keeping his voice low. 'A mean, ornery critter who causes most of the trouble in this town. The other two are called Nat and Lem, not the most popular fellers in Peaceful. Most people avoid that crowd like they got smallpox.'

'They don't look very savoury,' agreed Buck.

Just then the door opened again and Zeke returned, puffing happily at his brand-new corncob.

Bull Bartram sniggered and elbowed his lanky companion in the ribs.

'Look what's jist blowed in,' he sneered. 'A regular hill-billy if'n I ever see'd one.'

'Hello, gents,' said Zeke amiably. 'Nice day, ain't it?'

'No, it ain't,' disputed Bartram.

'Howzat?' A puzzled frown creased Zeke's brow.

'Fer one thing, we ain't had no

entertainment.' The BE foreman grinned maliciously, produced a stogie, lit it, and blew smoke up at Zeke's face.

'I reckon this hill-billy should be able to show us a pretty fair jig, don't you, boys?' Bartram winked at his partners.

'I don't dance,' Zeke said coldly.

'Looks like he'll need some persuadin', Bull,' said Nat, the thin one.

'That right, Hayseed? Want a little help to get yuh started?' Bartram reached for his guns, but never got there.

Moving with surprising speed for such a big man, Zeke took one step forward and smashed a huge fist into the foreman's beard. For a split second Bartram's eyes registered astonishment, then he lost interest in the proceedings as he toppled from his chair, slid across the floor, adopted a supine position, and commenced dreaming.

Nat and Lem went for their guns, but froze half-way as they found themselves staring into the business end of Buck's Colt.

24

'If'n you gents want to fight my friend,' Buck informed them, 'you jist put yore fists up. You can see he don't wear no gun.'

The BE punchers both expressed reluctance to tackle Zeke in that manner.

The poker players gathered round the prostrate form of Bull Bartram and examined him critically.

'Looks like he got a sudden case of the mumps,' Art Nelson diagnosed, pointing to a swelling materialising under the foreman's beard.

'I dunno about that,' opined Chuck Wiseman, 'but I shore bet his jaw is busted.'

'Hear that, you two?' said Buck to Nat and Lem. 'If there's a doctor in this town, I suggest yuh drag yore boss around to him an' get him fixed up. And tell the doc that he could get pretty busy if'n you *hombres* don't show more politeness to visitors.'

The two cowboys rose without a word, picked up the still sleeping foreman, and carried him outside.

'Good riddance,' muttered Slim Robinson as they left. 'Never could stand that BE crowd. Lemme buy you gents a drink, it's a long time since anyone stood up to Bull Bartram and his cronies.'

'They're already poured,' grinned the bartender. 'And these are on me.'

'Better watch yore step from now on, fellers,' warned Bart Keene. 'You shore made an enemy of the BE.'

'Yeah, they won't take kindly to what you done,' endorsed Chuck.

'Seems like yuh brought trouble on us again, Zeke,' sighed Buck, taking up his drink.

★　★　★

Buck and Zeke had to weather a round of drinks from every one of the cowpokes before they could escape out into the street.

'Phew!' said Buck as they made their way along the wooden sidewalk. 'We shore made ourselves popular with those boys!'

'Yeah,' grunted Zeke. 'And collected a hull lot of enemies at the same time.'

'Meanin' the BE crowd. Well, seems like they didn't want to be friends in the fust place. Mebbe it's better that way, at least we know where we stand. You go git beautified in the barber's shop,' grinned Buck.

Zeke entered the barber's and Buck crossed the street to where the sand-blasted, faded sign proclaimed: 'Peaceful Hotel'.

Inside, the dingy reception hall was no worse than dozens he had seen. The receptionist clambered to his feet as Buck entered, blinking sleep from his watery eyes.

'Got a room for me an' my pardner?' Buck tossed him a silver dollar. 'That's payment in advance, before you argue.'

'Yes, sir,' replied the receptionist. 'Nice double room, fust left up the stairs.'

'He's kinda big,' confessed Buck

euphemistically. 'Needs a somewhat larger than normal cot.'

'Our beds is big enough for giants,' the man said proudly. And then added optimistically, 'Half price if'n his feet stick out.'

'We'll take it,' said Buck, sensing a bargain.

Just then a thick-set man in his fifties, wearing a neat, pin-striped suit, grey derby and steel-rimmed spectacles, came down the stairs.

'Going out for a while,' he informed the receptionist. 'What time do you serve dinner?'

'Be about an hour, sir,' replied the receptionist, glancing at the clock on the wall.

The well-dressed man nodded to Buck and went outside.

'He ain't local, is he?' Buck asked the receptionist. 'Looks like a city gent to me.'

'No, he ain't local. Came in on the stage an hour or so ago.' The receptionist slid the register across to

Buck. 'Sign this, please.'

Buck signed for Zeke and himself, noting that the previous entry was signed 'Frank Smith'.

'Will yuh heat up some water, mister?' asked Buck. 'Me an' my pardner both need baths.'

'Shore. Name's Pete McCall.' He glanced at the register. 'Which one is you — Lawrence or Henderson?'

'I'm Buck Lawrence. Zeke'll be along soon.'

* * *

The dining-room was at the back of the hotel. Zeke and Buck had bathed, shaved and stabled their horses by the time dinner was ready. Frank Smith was already there when they entered.

'Hello, gents,' he greeted. 'Looks like we're the only diners.'

'Uh-huh.' Buck introduced Zeke and they sat down at the only table. The waiter brought well-filled plates and they set to with relish. Zeke, as usual, finished first and commented, 'Real aigs! I ain't had real aigs since I don't know when.'

'Travel about a lot, do you?' asked Smith. 'What line of work are you gents in?'

'We're dee-tectives,' lied Buck, taking a sip of coffee. 'Hmm. Arbuckle's best, if'n I ain't a hawg's uncle.'

Zeke shot him a puzzled look, but kept quiet.

Smith looked interested. 'Detectives, eh? Then you're just the people I'm looking for.'

Buck rolled himself a quirly and lit it. 'Yessir, jist about the best dang dee-tectives this side of the Mississippi.'

'Would you be willing to take the job of finding my son?' Smith asked.

'Depends where yuh lost him,' hedged Zeke, ramming tobacco into his corncob.

'Well, I haven't exactly lost him,' Smith admitted. 'Did you ever hear of Smith's Pickles?'

'Can't say as I have,' said Buck.

'Well, that's me. I got quite a successful business going over in Boston. Young Johnny was bored by it all, said he wanted some excitement in life. He left home for Texas some years ago. I used to hear from him from time to time, Arizona, New Mexico, Colorado. He drifted a lot as a cowpuncher. I hadn't heard from him since before my wife died last year, until I received this telegram a few days ago.'

'What did it say?' prompted Zeke.

'I didn't understand it fully. Said he'd been framed for a murder and needed help. The telegram was sent from Peaceful.'

'You come to the right place to start lookin',' Buck told him, drawing on his cigarette.

'Then you'll help me? Dollar a day, plus expenses.'

'Yeah, that's all right for jist findin' him. But if the law's after him for murder, you ain't much better off, are yuh? Mebbe we'll have to find the real killer or killers to git yore boy off the hook. That's worth a heap more, I'd say.'

Smith finished his coffee and thought for a while, doing some mental calculations.

'Five dollars a day, and not a cent more,' he said at length.

'Each,' prompted Buck.

'Yes, each,' sighed Smith. 'If you're the great detectives you claim to be, it shouldn't take you long.'

'Yuh never can tell,' Buck said non-committally. 'But I shouldn't be surprised if'n we ain't got a lead by mornin'. Mr. Smith, can yuh ride a hoss?'

'Just about, I guess. I've not done any riding for maybe twenty years, but I reckon I know enough not to fall off. Why?'

'I was wonderin' if'n you'd like to ride with us tomorrow. Yuh look kinda pale, the fresh air'll do yuh good.'

'Has this got anything to do with finding my son?'

'Could be. We've got a few inquiries to make this evenin'; we shore ain't gonna find him jist sittin' on our butts.'

'All right. See you in the morning then.'

'We'll set out right after breakfast.'

Frank Smith got up and left and Zeke turned to Buck, full of questions.

'What the hell was that all about? Where are we goin' tomorrow, an' how long have we been dee-tectives?'

'Jist about ten minutes, to answer yore last question fust,' grinned Buck. 'We've got ourselves a job, ain't we?'

'Could get us in a hull lot of trouble,' Zeke pointed out.

'Trouble's yore middle name, yuh overgrown galoot. We already know where Johnny worked, but I didn't want our employer to know that. Let him think we're startin' from scratch. Tomorrow we'll ride out to the PF ranch and see the widder. Tonight, we've gotta go back to the saloon an' find out where the ranch is. Got that, Mr. Dee-tective?'

'I got it,' Zeke answered.

* * *

There were a few fresh faces in the bar at the Bald Eagle when Buck and Zeke arrived. The Bar L punchers were at the card table again and chorused their greetings; the strangers gawped at Zeke's gigantic frame in the usual fashion.

Ed Williamson beamed. 'Howdy, gents. Didn't recognise yuh, Buck, without yore beard, but there's no forgettin' the big feller. What'll yuh have?'

'I'll have a beer, Ed,' said Zeke. 'An' some of that tonsil varnish for Buck, here.'

Still grinning, Ed poured the drinks.

'Folks,' he announced to all and sundry, 'these two here are yore actual conquerin' heroes. The ones the whole town is talkin' about.'

'Word shore gets around,' smiled Buck, taking up his whiskey.

'Shore does when Luke's in town,' chuckled Ed. 'That bow-legged jasper musta tole ev'ryone what you two did to Bull Bartram an' his polecats.'

'Got fixed up at the hotel?' inquired Duke Summerville.

'More'n that, Duke,' Zeke said. 'We got ourselves a job.'

'Already?' The Bar L man was amazed. 'You boys shore don't waste much time.'

'We're dee-tectives,' Zeke declared proudly.

Buck frowned. He wished he had warned the big ape to keep his mouth shut about that, but it was too late now. The less people knew about Frank Smith hiring them, the better. Now, with the town grapevine being what it was, everyone would know by morning.

'I shore never figgered you two for Pinkerton men,' said Ed, polishing the bar.

'Aw, we ain't Pinkertons,' Zeke explained. 'We've just been hired by Johnny Smith's pa. He nat'rally wants to find his boy.'

A burly man in a black stetson walked

over to them, twirling his moustache.

'I hope yuh don't intend obstructin' the law,' he said.

Ed jerked a thumb in the man's direction. 'This here is Hank Rawlins, boys. He's our sheriff.'

'Hello, Sheriff,' Buck nodded. 'We've no intention of hidin' him or anythin', if'n we find him. But it seems like there are some folks who don't think Johnny's guilty of murder. In that case, we're hired to find the real killer.'

'Well, let me know if you come up with anythin',' the sheriff said. 'At the moment, Johnny is top of the list of suspects. I'll admit I kinda liked the boy, but I gotta do my duty, an' the circumstantial evidence don't look too healthy for him.'

'Got any idea where he might be holin' up, Sheriff?' Buck inquired.

'No,' replied Hank. 'He's plumb disappeared. Mebbe he's out of the country by now. If'n he's guilty it's a shore bet.'

'He sent his pa a telegram sayin' it

was a frame up,' Buck told him. 'I guess that's the kinda thing an innocent man would do.'

'Hmm.' The sheriff looked thoughtful. 'Could be a cover-up, though. Mebbe he expected his pa to hire one o' them tricky lawyers from back East.'

'He hired us instead,' put in Zeke, lighting his pipe.

'Yeah,' Hank grinned. 'I hear you've already had a run-in with Bull Bartram. Better watch yoreselves, boys. That whole outfit don't take kindly to bein' pushed around. Even more so when it affects Bram Ewell.'

'Who's that? The boss?' asked Buck.

'That's right. Thinks mighty high of hisself, that one.'

'Sounds like they got the hull town scared of 'em,' remarked Zeke.

'If'n yo're suggestin' that includes me,' said Hank, 'yo're dead wrong. I've run a number of the BE punchers in a time or two for bein' drunk an' disorderly. But there ain't never been no serious crime I could pin on 'em.'

'Oh, well, I guess every town has a few drunks an' bad 'uns,' said Buck, dismissing the matter. 'What we really came to find out is where the PF ranch is.'

'Yuh take the north-east trail through the cottonwoods at the back of Joe's pool hall. It's about seven miles, I reckon.'

'Thanks, Sheriff,' said Buck. 'Can I get yuh a drink, yo're lookin' empty.'

Hank Rawlins accepted the drink, and the conversation drifted to cow country topics. A few more people came in, including Luke Simms, the stage driver, the only one whom Zeke and Buck had met before. None of the BE hands put in an appearance. The two newly-hired detectives left about eleven and returned to the hotel.

3

The next morning, after breakfast, they rode out with Frank Smith and followed the trail through the clump of cottonwoods, climbing a hill for nearly a mile and then coming out on the open range at the top.

'Mind telling me where we're going?' Smith asked after a while.

'Johnny was working for the PF ranch,' explained Buck. 'We're goin' to see the Widder Farrow, who owns the outfit. The murder took place at her ranch house.'

As they rode through the grassland, following the trail, Buck noted that, of the few cattle they saw, scarcely any bore the PF brand. Mostly they were BE stock, but there were some belonging to the Bar L. Another thing that struck him as unusual was that he saw no mavericks. At this time of year, with several cattle spreads around, there should be quite a few unbranded calves.

After an hour or so they topped a rise and saw the ranch nestling in a small valley before them. They rode up to the ranch house and Alice Farrow came out to meet them.

'Mornin', ma'am,' said Buck, touching his hat. 'This here is Frank Smith, Johnny's father, an' we're a couple of dee-tectives.'

Alice gave them a friendly, albeit tired, smile.

'Come on in, boys,' she said. 'I'll put the coffee on.'

They went in the house and sat down. When Alice returned from the kitchen, Frank Smith explained about the telegram he had received.

'We wondered if there was anything you could tell us that might help us to discover Johnny's whereabouts,' he said.

'I'm afraid not, Mr. Smith. As I've already told the sheriff, he just rode away after we found Dan's body. He didn't say where he was going.'

40

'You heard nothing else that night, besides the shot?' Buck inquired.

'Not a thing. It was all quiet, too quiet, perhaps.'

'Mrs. Farrow, do you think Johnny killed your foreman?' asked Smith.

Alice looked at him steadily. 'No, I don't, Mr. Smith. He was such a nice boy, and he had no reason to kill Dan. The two got on well together.'

'Is there anyone you suspect?' Buck put in. 'Somebody who had a grudge against him, perhaps. Or against Johnny?'

'No, there's nobody. I can't understand it at all.'

'There's a rider comin',' said Zeke, looking through the window.

Alice looked out and a frown creased her face.

'That's Bram Ewell,' she said. 'I can do without him pestering me at a time like this.'

Ewell dismounted and hitched his horse to the rail.

'Hello, Alice,' he said. 'I've come to

offer my condolences an' see if'n there's anythin' I can do.'

He was a big man, with dark, bushy eyebrows set under a Texas hat. At his hip he wore a Colt Navy .36.

'No, Mr. Ewell, I'm managing quite well, thank you.' Alice's voice had taken on a slightly icy edge. 'The sheriff and these gentlemen have matters well in hand.'

Ewell looked at Buck and then at Zeke, and his eyes hardened. The descriptions he had had from his men tallied with what he saw.

'You must be the bullies who beat up my foreman,' he snarled accusingly.

Buck looked at him levelly. 'You got that wrong, Mr. Ewell,' he said grimly. 'Bartram was pullin' a gun on Zeke, who was unarmed. Zeke hit him in self-defence.'

'That ain't the story I've heard,' Ewell grated.

'It's the one you'll hear from plenty witnesses in the Bald Eagle,' Buck asserted.

Ewell turned to Alice. 'I'll come again when you ain't got such bad company. I want to talk to you in private.' He mounted his horse and glared at Buck and Zeke, who had both come to the doorway.

'You two had better leave my boys alone, or there'll be more trouble than you can handle,' was his parting shot as he rode away.

'Not a very nice man,' commented Smith when they returned to the main room.

'He's a nuisance,' Alice said. 'He keeps coming round every few weeks since Pete died. He wants to court me, but I can't stand him. Oh, the coffee — '

She left the room and went into the kitchen, returning with four steaming cups on a tray.

'Thanks, ma'am,' said Smith, taking his cup first.

'Call me Alice,' she smiled. 'Everyone else does. I'm glad you boys were here, I'd have had a hard job getting rid of him otherwise. But watch out for him and his thugs. They're bad medicine.'

After they had drunk their coffees Buck said, 'Mind if we look around, ma'am?'

'Not at all,' she said. 'Come on, I'll show you.'

She led the way on to the porch. 'There's the spot where Dan was shot,' she said, pointing to a dark patch on the boards.

Buck walked around, examining the ground.

'What're we lookin' for, Buck?' whispered Zeke.

'Clues,' replied Buck. 'We're dee-tectives, yuh know.'

He bent down and picked up something from behind a bush, examining it critically.

'Did Dan or Johnny smoke stogies?' he asked Alice.

The widow pulled a face. 'No, they both rolled their own cigarettes.'

'Somebody's been around recently smokin' this,' Buck said, holding up a crushed cigar butt.

44

'Good place for an ambush, that bush,' remarked Zeke, feeling he should be contributing to the detective business. 'Especially in the dark.'

'Exactly,' Buck agreed. 'Any of yore callers smoke seegars, ma'am?'

'Not that I know of. Wait a minute, I think Bram Ewell does, but he's not been here for some time. That was his first call since Dan was shot.'

'When did it rain last?' asked Buck.

'Let's see now,' the widow thought for a moment. 'Oh, yes, there was a storm a couple of weeks ago. Lasted about an hour, heavy rain.'

Buck looked at the stogie. 'Dry as a bone,' he commented. 'If'n this had been in the rain, it would have deteriorated a lot more. It shore looks like the murderer was lyin' in wait, smokin' this for some time before anyone showed up.'

'That feller I hit was smokin' a stogie,' said Zeke, holding up a hamlike fist. 'It burnt me jist there.'

'I reckon there's a hull lot of fellers

45

that smoke 'em out here,' observed Buck. 'But if Johnny an' Dan rolled their own, this one shore belonged to somebody else.'

'That's not enough evidence to clear Johnny, is it?' Frank Smith reflected.

'No, it ain't,' Buck answered. He thought for a while, absent-mindedly rolling a cigarette.

'Go ahead and smoke,' smiled Alice. 'I don't mind, all the boys used to do it.'

'Thanks, Mrs. Farrow.' He lit up and looked at her. 'A bullet carries more weight than a seegar. Do yuh know what calibre slug killed yore foreman?'

'No, I don't, but they did an autopsy. The sheriff will know, won't he?'

'Yeah, he will. What kind of six-shooter did Johnny carry?'

'I can tell you that,' put in Smith. 'He bought a Whitney Navy revolver, a thirty-six, before he came out here. Said they used to use them on the Chisholm Trail. He always read a lot about the West before he left home.'

'Does he still use that gun, Mrs.

Farrow?' asked Buck.

'I think so, but I'm not too sure. I don't know an awful lot about guns. I just keep an old shotgun to keep off coyotes.'

'Seems like there's a few of the two-legged kind around these parts,' observed Zeke.

'How did your husband die, Mrs. Farrow — er — Alice?' Smith asked.

'He was shot with a rifle out on the western range. About three years ago.'

'Did they ever get the killer?'

'No, they never did. There was a bunch of desperadoes marauding about the ranches north of here. It was always assumed that they did it.'

'Do you think they did?'

She shrugged. 'Who knows? They were desperate men, on the run from the law. Perhaps Pete surprised them rustling, or something, and they just shot him.'

'Was Ewell here then?'

'Yes, he's been ranching here for about five years. Pete never got on with him, but he wasn't alone. None of the other ranchers have much to do with Bram Ewell.'

'The only other outfit we've come across is the Bar L,' Buck told her.

'Bill Langham's all right. Nice family. Margaret, his wife, gave me a lot of comfort when I lost Pete. They've a daughter, Kate. There are some other ranchers, but none near enough to come into contact much. Those up north of here, and to the west, go into Brent Creek for their supplies.'

'We know there's nothin' much to the south, 'cos we came in that way. Not good grazin' land at all, nothin' but brush, mesquite an' cactus.'

'We don't wish to impose on you, Alice,' said Smith, and then caught sight of Zeke's face, which had gone through emotions of delight and despair.

Buck stepped in to Zeke's rescue. 'I'm happy as I am, ma'am, but it's Zeke here. He's got this rare disease which makes him eat all the time. If'n he don't get fed for a few hours, he jist plumb withers away.'

Alice smiled. 'You mean he's always hungry. I can see he's got a mighty big frame to fill. You all just sit there, while I rustle something up.'

After lunch, they said their goodbyes and rode off towards Peaceful.

'Mighty nice lady, that,' commented Zeke, as they went through the ranch gate.

'Yes, she sure is,' agreed Smith. 'Reminds me of my wife, in some ways.'

'Well, if'n yo're stayin' out here for some time, mebbe you'll get to know her a little better,' said Buck.

'I sure hope so,' was Smith's reply.

★ ★ ★

Duke Summerville was in his customary position, propping up the bar at the Bald Eagle, when Buck and Zeke went in that evening.

'Howdy, boys,' he greeted. 'How's the dee-tectin' business? Come up with anythin' yet?'

Buck grinned. 'Give us time, Duke,' he said, as the bartender poured their drinks. 'It might take us a day or two to wrap this one up.'

'Yeah. Guess it's a big country to find jist one man.'

Buck rolled a cigarette, lit it, and blew smoke thoughtfully. 'I been tryin' to think of a motive, more than Johnny's whereabouts. He'll turn up presently, I'm shore o' that. An' then there was Pete Farrow's murder, they never got nobody for that. Mebbe the two are connected.'

'Johnny was with us when Pete got shot,' replied Duke. 'He's got a cast-iron alibi for that one.'

'I wasn't thinkin' about Johnny,' Buck reflected. 'I meant that the reasons Pete an' Dan Beardow got killed could be the same.'

'Somebody has it in for the PF ranch? That could mean that Johnny is next in line, couldn't it?'

'Could be,' admitted Buck. 'But we were out at the PF today, an' Mrs.

Farrow ain't the sort to make enemies. Anybody ever show any interest in buyin' the ranch?'

'Not that I know of,' said Duke.

'Shore ain't got much stock,' supplied Zeke. 'Can't be worth much at the moment.'

Buck looked at his partner in admiration. So he, too, had noticed the paucity of PF brands on their ride out to the ranch.

Buck turned back to Duke. 'About three years ago, when Pete Farrow was killed, what was cattle fetchin' at the Kansas stockyards?'

Duke thought for a moment. 'Lemme see, yearlin's and two-year-olds would be around seventeen dollars a head, three-year-olds nineteen dollars. But Farrow had a mixed stock, Aberdeen Angus, short-horns an' even a few Durhams. They would be worth up to sixty dollars at, say, Abilene or Dodge City.'

'Did Farrow ship any cattle the year he got killed?'

51

'Shore did. Herd of around a thousand, I'd say.'

'An' did he hire, or take 'em up himself?'

'Dan Beardow was his trail boss. Pete went up to the stockyards an' met him there. He liked to do the actual sellin' hisself.'

Buck thought for a moment. 'So, with no trail margin, he probably netted upwards of twenty thousand dollars.'

'What are yuh gettin' at, Buck?' asked Zeke, stuffing tobacco into his corncob.

'I was wonderin' if'n Mrs. Farrow ever got hold of that money,' replied Buck.

'Well, she shore ain't done any restockin' since,' observed Duke. 'Been runnin' the ranch on a shoestring. She couldn't afford to keep the hands on. I think Dan stayed out of friendship, an' Johnny would work for next to nothin', if'n he got his meals free.'

'An' Mrs. Farrow shore is a good cook,' chuckled Zeke.

Just then the door opened and Hank

Rawlins came in, accompanied by a lank, lean individual wearing a Plainsman hat and a morose face, looking as though it had seen all the troubles of the world, and then some. They walked over to the bar and Hank ordered whiskeys.

'Howdy, Sheriff,' greeted Buck. 'Who's yore friend?'

The sheriff took a quick drink. 'This here is Moose Roberts, my deputy.'

Moose nodded. 'Been hearin' how you gents roughed up Bull Bartram. If'n yo're lookin' for trouble, yo're shore goin' the right way to find it.'

Buck grinned. 'So we've heard. Say, Sheriff, what calibre bullet was it that killed Dan Beardow?'

'Thirty-six,' answered the sheriff. 'Why, are yuh on to somethin'?'

'No, jist curious.'

Moose was looking awe-stricken at Zeke.

'Yore pardner there, is he a mountain man?' he asked Buck.

Buck grinned again. 'No, he jist looks

that way. More a man-mountain, I'd say.'

The others laughed, but Zeke was offended. 'I ain't a orniment,' he told them. 'I can answer for myself, Mr. Roberts. Yuh don't have to use this lame-brain as an interpreter. If'n yuh want to ask me somethin', go ahead an' ask me.'

'Yessir,' gulped Moose, 'I'll shore remember that.'

★ ★ ★

After breakfast the next day, Buck and Zeke saddled up and left town on the same trail they had ridden the day previously.

As they climbed the hill behind the cottonwoods, Zeke asked, 'Why are we goin' this way again, Buck? We covered this range yesterday.'

Buck countered with a question of his own. 'Would yuh rather eat in the hotel, or try some more of Mrs. Farrow's fried chicken an' apple pie?'

Zeke grinned. 'No contest,' he said.

When they reached the mesa, Buck nodded to the left. 'We'll take a different route this time, I wanna look around at the cattle on this range.'

'Lookin' for evidence of rustlin', I suppose,' suggested Zeke.

'There's been no round-up on the PF for three years. What few cattle were left after the last one should have increased somewhat in that time. If'n they ain't, then it shore points to some funny business.'

They rode around in a wide arc, north for a couple of miles and then east. The first cow they saw was a two-year-old, and examination showed it to be bearing the BE brand. A few hundred yards further on they came across a group of half a dozen. One of them was a calf of a few months old with no brand, the others were all BE. After an hour's riding they had spotted three mavericks and twenty-five BE steers. Buck called a halt and they sat down in the shade of a cottonwood.

Buck drew his tobacco pouch and rolled a quirly. Zeke lit his corncob and they reviewed the situation.

'One wouldn't think that there was a PF ranch at all,' Buck reflected. 'The only mavericks we've seen all obviously belong to BE cows.'

'I suppose we could be pretty close to the BE range up here,' Zeke pointed out. 'Mebbe all the PF critters are on the eastern range.'

'I wonder if the PF's done any brandin' since Pete Farrow died?' Buck pondered.

'Dan Beardow was a tophand, an' lately he's had Johnny helpin' him. It shore is strange if'n they never got around to brandin' a few critters in all that time.'

'Yeah,' agreed Buck. 'Murder an' rustlin'. An' they call this valley Peaceful.'

They sat for a while in silence, finishing their smokes. Then Buck looked at the sun and grinned at his partner. 'If'n I know yore stummick, it should be startin' to holler for vittles about now, eh?'

'I've heard of readin' minds, Buck, but I'll be hornswoggled if'n I'd heard of readin' stummicks before,' said Zeke, rising to his feet. 'Yo're right, though. I could eat a fried mule, sunnyside up.'

They mounted and headed across rough country in the direction they decided the ranch must lie. After about ten minutes, Buck's wary eyes detected the glint of sun on metal from behind a brush clump a hundred yards to their left.

'Head for those boulders, quick,' he ordered Zeke.

The big man recognised the urgency in Buck's tone and spurred his horse to a sudden gallop. Buck followed as a shot rang out. They reached the cluster of boulders as two more bullets zipped through the air behind them. Buck seized his Winchester as he dropped to cover. A bullet chipped the huge boulder as they lay panting behind it.

'They musta followed us from town,' Zeke gasped.

'Yeah, an' decided we was becomin' too nosey.'

Buck could just glimpse the clump of brush between two large boulders. He loosed a shot at it and had the satisfaction of hearing a yell.

'Did yuh hit one of 'em?' asked Zeke.

'Dunno. Can't see anybody out there. Musta been close enough to scare 'em, though.'

Several more shots clipped the rocks, but the two cowboys were well sheltered from any ricochet. Buck watched the narrow space between the boulders, and after a while saw a tall hat moving slightly. His Winchester barked and the hat flew into the air. There was a flurry of movement among the brush as though several men were shifting positions. Buck emptied his rifle into the brush and withdrew behind the boulder to reload.

'They shore are amateurs,' he observed, pushing bullets into the empty chambers. 'There's open space further on where they could have had us for shore.'

'Yeah,' agreed Zeke. 'I reckon we're in a better position here than they are out there. That brush might hide 'em, but it shore won't stop bullets.'

Buck poked his rifle through the crack again.

'They're leavin',' he announced. 'Three of 'em, high-tailin' behind that brush as fast as their hosses'll move.'

He stood up and fired twice at the fleeing ambushers. Then he turned and grinned at Zeke. 'Hope that little fracas didn't put yuh off yore dinner, pardner,' he said, dusting himself down with his hat.

'Not on yore life, it jist gave me a edge to my appetite, Buck,' Zeke replied.

'I figger they've got too much a head start for us to go chasin' 'em,' Buck said, as he mounted his pinto. 'I wonder who them varmints are.'

'A dollar to a plugged nickel they're connected with the rustlin',' Zeke ventured. 'But that don't necessarily make 'em the killers, too.'

'Wish I knew if'n I hit one of 'em,' growled Buck. 'All I know is that I ventilated a hat.'

'Let's go take a look at that brush patch,' suggested Zeke. 'Mebbe they left a corpse behind.'

They rode over to where the ambushers had been hiding and conducted a careful search.

'Nothin' here,' announced Buck disgustedly. 'No sign of blood. The *hombre* who almost got his hair parted even took his punctured hat.'

★ ★ ★

Less than an hour later they pulled up at the PF ranch. Mrs. Farrow came out to greet them.

'Hello, boys,' she said. 'Is Mr. Smith not with you today?' She sounded a little disappointed.

'No, ma'am, he ain't,' answered Buck. 'An' it's a good thing, too. We was dry-gulched on the way out here.'

'An ambush!' she gasped. 'Did either of you get hurt?'

'No, ma'am, not a scratch,' said Zeke. 'But we ain't so shore about the bushwhackers,' he added.

'Come on in and make yourselves at home,' Alice invited. 'If you care to try some of my stew, there's hot biscuits to follow.'

Zeke winked at Buck and smacked his lips. 'Shore sounds appetisin', ma'am,' he said as they entered the ranch house and sat down. 'Come to think of it, I am a bit peckish.'

Alice laughed. 'Judging by the amount you ate yesterday, it's a wonder you've any room yet for some more.'

'Seems like there's allus room for more in Zeke, ma'am,' Buck informed her. 'Yuh see, he's got holler laigs.'

After they had finished the last of the biscuits, Zeke leaned back in his chair and smiled blissfully.

'I reckon I ain't never tasted better grub than that, ma'am,' he said, 'an' I've et in some fancy eatin' houses in my time.'

'Why, thank you,' Alice said, blushing slightly. 'Did you boys come over just to sample my cooking, or was there something else?'

'Partly that, partly somethin' else,' Buck said. 'It's a bit embarrassin', what we want to ask yuh.'

Alice looked puzzled. 'Embarrassing? Well, go ahead and ask,' she told him. 'Anything that will help convict Dan's murderer. I don't believe that Johnny did it, as I told you yesterday.'

'I think there's a connection between the killing of yore husband an' yore foreman's murder, but I'm durned if'n I can see what it is.'

'It's three years since Pete was killed,' Alice reminded him. She was still frowning.

'Yeah, but I figger that somebody has got designs on this ranch, an' is mebbe tryin' to scare yuh off. Anybody made yuh an offer for the ranch since then?'

'No. But it wouldn't be worth much,

there's very little stock here nowadays.'

'Yore husband made a cattle drive three years ago, so I'm told,' Buck went on. 'D'yuh know how many head he sold?'

'No, but it was a big herd for him. Dan was tally man. I never took much interest in the cattle business myself.'

Buck took a deep breath. 'How about the money from that drive? There must have been quite a lot involved.'

'Yes, I suppose there was, but as I said, I didn't have anything to do with it.'

'Was there a big amount for you in yore husband's will?'

Alice smiled. 'I see what you mean about being embarrassed. No, he never left a will. He didn't trust banks much, but there was a few thousands in the bank at Peaceful, and a few dollars in his pockets.'

'But nothin' like twenty thousand, huh?'

'Oh, goodness, no. Nothing like that amount.'

'And since then?'

'We've just managed to survive. I like it out here, and don't want to leave unless I'm forced to.'

'Have yuh got the tally sheets for that last round-up, Mrs. Farrow?'

'Oh, yes. Just a moment.'

She went over to a large oak bureau and searched for a few moments. 'Here's the book. Have a look for yourself.'

Buck took the tally book and scanned the last few pages. Satisfied, he handed the book back to Alice.

'Thank yuh, ma'am,' he said. 'Do yuh know there's twenty-three thousand dollars not accounted for?'

Alice gasped. 'Twenty-three thousand? I could never understand that book. Are you sure?'

'Yes, ma'am,' replied Buck. 'Any idea where it might be?'

'No, I've no idea where he kept the money.'

'Have yuh searched the ranch thoroughly?'

'Well,' she admitted, 'I did have a look around after the funeral, but I never found anything. I'd no idea that amount was missing.'

'When we're gone, you go through everythin' with a toothcomb. I'm layin' odds that money is cached away somewheres.'

'I'll certainly have a good look now. Gosh! That would mean I could hire hands and buy some stock again.'

'I should be mighty particular who you hire, Mrs. Farrow. Have yuh any suspicion of rustlin'?'

'Rustling? No.'

'Would Dan or Johnny mention it if they noticed anythin'?'

Alice rubbed her chin thoughtfully. 'They never did,' she said. 'But maybe they wouldn't like to worry me about that. Why, do you think there's been rustlers around?'

'Until we get some evidence, ma'am, we ain't sayin' anythin' either. You jist leave it to us.'

4

'What's next?' asked Zeke as they rode away from the PF ranch.

'As I see it,' drawled Buck, 'we got a choice. Either we ride over to the Bar L to see Bill Langham, or we see if'n we can get some evidence from one o' these steers masqueradin' as BE cows.'

'Yuh mean rope an' kill one an' skin it, or ask it politely if'n it remembers bein' decorated with a runnin' iron after the regular brandin'?'

Buck went along with the sarcasm. 'As I recall, these steers have mighty poor memories. A piece o' hide with the brand obviously altered would stand up better in court than a dumb cow's testimony.'

'I thought yuh said we weren't doin' no more ropin' this year — we're dee-tectives now, remember?'

'Awright, Zeke, have it yore way. We'll

go an' see Langham.'

'No, let's get it over with. But do we have to kill a steer?'

'Unless yuh want to crawl down its throat an' take a look from the inside,' Buck suggested. 'But yuh better take some matches — it's awful dark in there.'

Zeke, realising he had lost the argument, jammed his sombrero firmly on his head and remained silent. A look of pity crossed Buck's features as he glanced at his companion.

'Yuh never did like that part of punchin', did yuh, pardner? Why don't yuh go over an' see what yuh can find at the Bar L an' leave the grisly bit to me?'

Zeke brightened up at that suggestion. 'Good idea, it'll save time. What d'yuh think I should ask 'em, Buck?'

'See if any of their cattle are missin'. Want to take my Winchester?'

'Naw, I'm likely to shoot my foot off. Ain't never needed a gun. But yuh seem more concerned with rustlin'. We been hired to find Johnny Smith, ain't we?'

'Shore, but I figger the rustlin' is connected with his frame-up. Yuh never know, yuh might jist run into Johnny while yo're over there.' Buck gave his partner a look which could have meant anything.

'Let's see,' said Zeke, 'we're north-east of town here, the BE is north-west of the PF, the south is all wasteland. I reckon the Bar L must be west of Peaceful somewheres. I'll ride into town an' check.'

'You do that, pardner. I'll see yuh tonight.'

Zeke rode away at a fast canter, leaving Buck to start searching for a likely candidate for skinning.

★ ★ ★

Kate Langham rode the grey mare at an easy trot into the strip of rough country which formed the eastern boundary of the Bar L. She was a pretty girl, no more than twenty, with corn-coloured hair, big blue eyes and a cute nose, sprinkled with freckles. Having run low on coffee at the ranch, and everyone else being busy, she had ridden into Peaceful for a fresh supply, which was slung in her saddlebags. As they did not need anything else, she had ridden her own horse instead of taking the buckboard.

As she made her way into a dry *coulée* she spotted a rider approaching. A glance was enough, there was no mistaking the flabby pear-shaped figure of Lem Ritchie, one of the BE's cow-punchers. She looked around for a means of avoiding him, but she was already too far into the narrow ravine, and in any case he had seen her. She rode on with apparent unconcern, but her distaste was evident in her eyes and the set of her mouth. She did not like any of the BE outfit, this one least of all.

When they were a few yards apart, Ritchie pulled his mount across, barring her path, and tipped his sombrero to the back of his head.

'Howdy, Miss Kate,' he said. 'Been to the store in town?'

'It's no concern of yours where I've been,' she replied acidly. 'Please let me by.'

He ignored the rebuke. 'Shore must get lonesome for yuh out here since that murderer took off.'

Kate's face turned crimson at the undisguised reference to Johnny Smith. 'He's not a murderer,' she blurted. 'And it's none of your business. Now get out of my way.'

Ritchie's piglike eyes narrowed. 'That's not a very polite way to speak to a neighbour,' he said, an edge entering his voice. He drew his horse up to Kate's mare. 'Now, if'n yuh jist give me a little — '

He broke off at the sound of hooves pounding along the trail. Whirling round, he recognised the huge figure of Zeke heading towards them at a fast trot. Whipping out one of his six-guns, he pointed it at the oncoming colossus.

'Hold it right there, Hill-billy,' he snarled.

Zeke drew his mount to a halt some

ten yards away. 'Is this sidewinder botherin' you, Miss?' he called.

'Yes, he is,' Kate replied. 'But watch out for his gun.'

Zeke was already heeding the warning, keeping one wary eye on Ritchie's weapon while searching frantically for a means of disarming him.

Even at that distance, Zeke's sheer size in the saddle unnerved the BE man. 'Get down off'n that bronc,' he ordered. Looking down the trail and seeing and hearing no-one else, his confidence returned.

'So yuh ain't got yore gunslingin' pardner with yuh, eh?' he sneered as Zeke dismounted. 'Well, yuh jist wait there while I finish my business with this gal. Then I'll have a little fun with yuh.'

He turned back to Kate, who struck him in the mouth with the back of her hand. He started, his horse reared, and in the confusion Zeke grabbed a rock from the ravine floor. Kate backed her horse away, putting more space between

71

her and Ritchie. Zeke seized the opportunity and let fly with the rock.

His aim was a little high, but quite effective. As Lem Ritchie fought to control his mount, his head twisted round and he received a glancing blow on the temple, knocking him clean from his horse.

Zeke ran up to Kate. 'Are yuh all right, ma'am?' he asked.

'Yes, thank you,' she smiled with relief. 'You'd better make sure he's harmless.'

Zeke turned to the prostrate figure on the ground. In falling, the puncher's head had received another blow which had rendered him unconscious. A trickle of blood ran from the wound, but did not look too serious to Zeke.

'He'll live, I'm afraid, ma'am,' he said. Picking up Ritchie's fallen six-gun, he emptied it and put the shells in his pocket. Then he did the same with the one still in his gunbelt, and a quick search revealed yet another gun, a .41 calibre Remington two-barrel derringer, in a shoulder holster under his vest.

'Not a very trusting soul, is he?' Kate remarked, looking down.

'No, an' I ain't trustin' him not to wait for me comin' back, ma'am,' replied Zeke, pocketing the last of the shells. He whistled his horse and remounted. 'We'll leave him there to rest awhile. He looks kinda peaceful.'

'You must be Zeke,' said Kate as they rode away. 'Duke Summerville told me about you, especially the episode with Bull Bartram.'

'Yes'm, that's me,' replied Zeke. 'I was jist ridin' over to see Bill Langham. Say, is he yore pa?'

'That's right, I'm Kate Langham. Where's Buck Lawrence, your partner?'

'He's attendin' to a little business on the PF range, ma'am. They've been losin' cows. Have yuh been missin' any of yore stock?'

'No. If there's rustlers around, they've left us alone.'

As they rode on to Bar L rangeland, Zeke noticed that what Kate said was true. There were plenty of cattle around bearing the Bar L brand. He wondered if it was because the Bar L brand was more difficult to alter, but decided that there was probably more to it than that. After all, if a rustler wanted to steal stock he'd do it anyway. The penalty was the same, no matter whose cattle he stole.

'What was it you wanted to see Dad about, Zeke?' Kate asked him as they neared the ranch.

'Waal, me an' Buck, we've been hired by Johnny Smith's pa to find his son, an' we reckon anythin' anyone can tell us about him might be useful. He used to work for the Bar L, didn't he?'

Kate shot him a quick look and flushed slightly. 'Yes, that's right. I'm sure he'd never shoot anyone in the back, let alone a nice man like Dan Beardow.'

'That's what everyone keeps tellin' us, ma'am. But somebody did, that's for shore.'

Zeke followed Kate into the ranch

house and was introduced to her parents. Bill Langham was a stocky individual, with a broad smile and twinkling eyes. He shook hands warmly with Zeke when Kate told him of the encounter with Lem Ritchie and Zeke's subsequent rescue. His wife, Margaret, was a slim, alert woman, who looked hardly old enough to be Kate's mother.

Over coffee, Zeke told them briefly what Buck and he had been doing since arriving in Peaceful. There were not many gaps in Langham's knowledge, Duke Summerville having kept him informed of events. He had not known about the ambush, however, nor Alice Farrow's missing twenty-three thousand dollars.

'You boys had better keep on your toes,' Langham warned. 'Whoever's behind all this won't stop at one murder.'

'Yuh don't think Johnny Smith killed Dan Beardow then?' Zeke probed.

Langham snorted. 'I know damn' well he didn't. Them two was friends an' were on the trail of the rustlers, jist like you an' your pardner.'

'Who tole yuh that?' asked Zeke.

Langham hesitated for a moment, and before he could reply a door to the hallway opened and a tall, rangy cowhand appeared.

'I did,' he said levelly, his eyes fixed on Zeke.

'Johnny!' gasped Margaret Langham. 'Now you've done it!'

'I don't think so, ma'am,' said Johnny Smith, stepping into the room. 'I think we can trust this feller to keep our secret. I've been listenin' to him behind the door, an' I think him an' his pardner are on our side.'

'Yo're Johnny Smith?' Zeke asked, a puzzled frown creasing his features.

'Yeah. And these good folks have been shelterin' me. Are yuh gonna turn me in?'

Zeke shook his head. 'Like you said, we'll keep yore secret. I guess it won't hurt the sheriff none if'n he jist stays iggerant of yore whereabouts.'

Johnny grinned. 'I figgered that if Pa trusts yuh, I can too. How is he? What does he reckon to the Wild West?'

'He's fine, Johnny,' replied Zeke. 'I reckon he's took a shine to some of the folks out here. Well, one at least.'

'Good. Tell him I'm doin' fine, will yuh? I'd shore like to see him.'

'I'm afraid that ain't possible yet, Johnny,' said Bill Langham. 'You can't come out of hidin' yet, they'll arrest yuh at least, an' mebbe some of the wilder crowd will be hankerin' for a necktie party.'

'He's right,' Zeke agreed. 'We'll bring yore pa out here to you. That's safer than havin' you gallivantin' about fer all to see.'

'Yeah, I suppose yo're right,' said Johnny. 'But it shore would feel good to be able to ride to town again. Not that I haven't enjoyed stayin' here,' he added, with a quick glance at Kate.

'We know what you mean, Johnny,' said Bill Langham. 'Must feel like a caged animal after ridin' the range.'

'You'll stay for supper?' Margaret asked Zeke.

'Now yuh mention it, ma'am, it is a while since I et. Guess I can find room fer a little snack.'

Margaret smiled and disappeared into the kitchen.

★ ★ ★

Later that evening Zeke found Buck in the hotel dining-room, just finishing a meal. Across the table from him was a lean, whiskery man who stared vacantly at Zeke as he entered the room.

'Hi, Zeke,' greeted Buck. 'Meet Repeater Riley. Repeater, this is my pardner, Zeke.'

Zeke nodded and Repeater grinned with his mouth, his eyes still keeping their vacant look.

'Repeater works for the BE,' explained Buck. 'Have yuh ordered supper, Zeke?'

'No, I ain't hungry. Got filled up back at the Bar L.' Zeke watched fascinatedly at Buck's companion wolfing at his piled-up plate.

Buck grinned. 'That's his third helpin' of cackleberries an' sowbelly,' he explained. 'I reckon Repeater could give yuh a run for yore money at eatin', Zeke. You shore you ain't hungry? I ain't never knowed you when yuh refused a meal.'

'Mrs. Langham shore cooks a fine meal, Buck,' said Zeke. 'I'll have to take yuh out there sometime.'

'Yeah, I'd like that. When yuh get through that lot, Repeater, we'll mosey over to the saloon an' we'll see how yuh like Ed's likker.'

'Yeah,' Repeater looked up and licked his lips. 'I shore would like a drink. Shore would. Thanks, Mr. Lawrence. Thanks.'

'Not at all. Yuh gotta kinda lonely job out there, wranglin' an' doin' odd jobs. It'll do yuh good to meet some o' the boys from the other ranches. They seem a mean lot at the BE.'

'No, Mr. Lawrence. They treat me

real good. Real good. Gave me a job when nobody else would. A job, that's what they gave me.' It was easy to see why he was called Repeater.

'All the same,' went on Buck, 'I shouldn't think Bull Bartram treats yuh very well. He's got a reputation for bein' ornery.'

'Bull's no back-shooter,' said Repeater, shovelling bacon into his mouth. 'No, suh, he's no back-shooter.'

'Who said he was?' Buck shot back at him keenly.

'No back-shooter.'

'How about them others — Nat an' Lem?'

'Nat Cross never done me no harm. No harm.'

'I had a run-in with the fat one today,' remarked Zeke. 'Nasty character.'

'Uh-huh.' Repeater looked around the room fearfully. 'Yuh won't tell nobody, huh?'

'Tell 'em what, Repeater?' asked Buck.

'The fat one — Lem — he done hit

me onct. Hit me. All I did was sit in his place in the mess hall. Hit me, no reason.'

Repeater crammed in the last mouthful and pushed his plate away. 'Have that drink now, eh? Shore am thirsty.'

'Shore. Wait here jist a minute, will yuh? I want to get something from my room.'

'All right, Mr. Lawrence. I'll wait right here. Right here.'

Buck walked over to the stairs where Zeke joined him.

'What yuh left upstairs, Buck?' the giant asked.

'Nothin'. That was an excuse to talk to you. What did yuh learn at the Bar L? Besides the fact that Mrs. Langham cooks a fine meal.'

'Johnny Smith is stayin' there.'

Buck pursed his lips and nodded slightly. 'I had a hunch he might be. Did yuh see him?'

'Shore. He's fine. His pa will be mighty pleased when we tell him.'

'Don't be in such a dad-blamed

hurry, big fella. We don't want to put ourselves outa work that quick. We gotta get to the bottom of the rustlin' an' killin' that's been goin' on around here.'

'As you say, Buck. Did yuh get the evidence?'

Buck grinned and drew a piece of hide from his pocket.

'See that,' he said, showing Zeke the BE brand. 'Now look at the other side.'

Zeke turned the hide over and saw a clear PF with a fresher loop to the P and a bar to the F, turning it into BE.

'Easy, ain't it?' continued Buck. 'An' I got me Repeater Riley, too.'

'Where does he come in?'

'He hangs around the BE all the time. He must see a lot that goes on there, but he's kinda dull-witted. We're gonna get him likkered up at the Bald Eagle, an' mebbe he'll talk. I think he's afraid of losin' his job an' when he's sober he's jist about got enough sense to stay quiet about the BE crowd.'

'And Ed's whiskey might loosen his tongue, eh?'

'That's right, Zeke. C'mon, let's get back to him.'

There were about a dozen customers in the bar, including the Bar L crowd at the poker table and Duke Summerville talking to Moose Roberts, the deputy sheriff. Ed Williamson, the bartender, dropped his jaw and wiped some froth from his moustache when he saw Buck and Zeke come in with Repeater.

'Well, I'll be hornswoggled!' he exclaimed. 'If'n it ain't Repeater Riley. What brings you to town, Repeater?'

'Ugh?' Repeater looked blankly at Ed, and then at the chandelier over the bar as if for inspiration. 'Er, Mr. Lawrence here, he brung me. Yeah, that's right. He brung me. Gonna buy me a drink.'

Buck smiled. 'That's right, Ed. Give Repeater whatever he wants. Then fill 'em up all round.'

Ed got busy. 'Celebratin' somethin', Buck?'

'No, not yet, Ed. Jist relaxin' after a good day's work.'

'Uh-huh. Found some clues, eh?'

'Mebbe.'

Moose Roberts picked up his drink and walked over to them. 'Anythin' I oughta know about, cowboy?'

Buck gazed thoughtfully at Moose for a moment, and then pulled out the piece of hide and handed it to the deputy.

'What d'yuh make of that, Moose?'

Moose took the hide and examined it. His eyebrows lifted and he twirled his moustache absently. Then he handed it back to Buck. 'Looks like shady business to me. Where'd yuh get it?'

'Oh, around,' said Buck, pocketing the hide. Then he changed the subject. 'Any of the BE boys been in lately, Ed?'

Ed chuckled. 'Ain't see'd hide nor hair of 'em since the shindig the other day. But don't be surprised if'n they ain't in tomorrow. Them boys ain't missed a Sat'dy night ever, less'n they been in jail.'

''Nother drink fer Repeater, Ed,' ordered Buck. 'He's gotta lot of supper to wash down, ain't that right, ol' pal?'

Repeater grinned. 'That's right, Mr. Lawrence. Wash down me supper. Ha! ha! Wash it down!'

'Can't have yuh buyin' all night, Buck,' said Duke. 'This one's on me.'

They plied Repeater with drinks until the effect was noticeable. Repeater did not have much opportunity for drinking and when he found himself in a saloon he endeavoured to make up for that sad fact. Nevertheless, his capacity was limited and his speech soon became slurred. Buck decided to try to get some sense out of him before he became too unintelligible.

'Ever see any signs of rustlin', Repeater?' he asked, rolling a cigarette.

'Rushlin'? Naw, no rushlin'. Seen plenty cowsh branded, though. Lotsa cowsh branded.' Repeater giggled inanely and chawed tobacco.

'D'yuh know Bram Ewell pretty well?' Buck lighted his cigarette.

'Fine fella, Bram Ewell. Gimme a job, he did. A job.'

'How about Pete Farrow? Did yuh know him?'

Repeater looked blank. 'Pete Farrow? Oh, yesh, I knowed him. Pete Farrow. Got hisself shot. Knew Lije Guthrie, too. Me, I'm clever. Don't talk about it. Keep m'job. Yesh, suh.'

It was Buck's turn to look blank. He turned to Duke. 'Who's he talkin' about, Duke?'

'Lije Guthrie was a cowhand at the BE. He disappeared jist after Pete was killed. Nobody ever heard from him since. Nor find his body,' Duke added ominously.

Buck turned back to a glassy-eyed Repeater, who by now was having difficulty staying upright.

'Do yuh know what happened to Guthrie, Repeater?' he asked, grasping the drunken wrangler by the shoulders.

'Who? Whashat?' Repeater tried desperately to focus on Buck's face.

'Lije Guthrie. What happened to him?'

Comprehension dawned for a moment in Repeater's bloodshot eyes. 'Oh, yeah. Lije Guthrie. Dishappeared. That's what he done. Jist dishappeared.'

'Where to?'

'Dunno. Tha'sh right. I'm shmart. Shmarter'n hell. Keep m'job.'

'Yuh know yuh can go to jail fer withholdin' information, don'tcha?'

'Jail? Ain't never been to jail. Awful places, jails. Ain't goin' to jail. Keep m'job.'

'We ain't gonna get no sense oughta him tonight, Buck,' remarked Zeke. 'He's too far gone.'

'One last try,' Buck sighed, drawing heavily on his cigarette. 'Now, Repeater. Do Bram Ewell or Bull Bartram know anythin' about Farrow or Guthrie?'

'Bull'sh no back-shooter,' murmured Repeater, as he slid gently to the floor. His eyes closed and he was snoring within seconds.

'Can't take the likker,' commented Duke. 'What do we do with him now?'

'Got a room here, Ed?' asked Buck.

'I'll pay for him as I'm responsible for his condition.'

Ed nodded. 'I can fix him up for the night, Buck. Give him breakfast if'n he needs any. Jist help me drag him through.'

'I'll do it,' volunteered Zeke, raising the hapless Repeater by the collar and hoisting him to shoulder height.

'What did he mean about Bull bein' no back-shooter?' asked Duke as Zeke disappeared behind the bar with his load.

'He kept sayin' that back in the hotel,' replied Buck. 'I think he means that somebody else is.'

'I wonder if he knows who that somebody is?'

'Well, we shore won't find that out tonight. Have another drink?'

5

It was not just the BE boys who came to town on a Saturday. It seemed like the whole county had arrived by the time Buck and Zeke went down to breakfast. All the hitch-rack space along the main street had been taken, the women were doing their shopping and the Bald Eagle was already bursting with cowboys. Even the dogs joined in the spirit, barking and fighting among themselves to add to the general racket.

Buck winced as he sat down at the breakfast table.

'Yuh'd think they'd have a little respect for us drinkers,' he said to Zeke. 'Dunno where they got the name 'Peaceful' from.'

Zeke grinned mercilessly and tucked into his bacon and eggs.

'Bet yore haid ain't as sore as poor ol' Repeater's,' he said. 'But there was no cause for yuh to carry on after he passed out. Yuh didn't learn no more after yuh learned that Bull's no back-shooter.'

Despite his throbbing temple, Buck managed a grin. 'He was kinda emphatic about that, wasn't he? Mebbe he saw Bull shoot somebody in the front once — they could wind up just as dead thataway.'

Frank Smith joined them at the table.

'Mornin', boys,' he greeted breezily. 'Never saw you yesterday. Out on the trail early?'

'Uh-huh,' Buck nodded. 'We collected a piece more evidence.'

'Any notion where Johnny might be?'

'Well,' said Buck, glancing at Zeke, 'I did get a message from him. He says he's fine an' yo're not to worry 'bout him.'

'Gee, that's great!' Smith smiled and sipped his coffee. 'I suppose he still wants to remain in hiding. Until you boys find the real killer, eh?'

'Yeah, that's about it,' Zeke agreed.

Smith looked out of the window.

'I was thinking of visiting Alice — er — Mrs. Farrow, today,' he said, 'but it seems like everyone has come to town. Maybe she has, too.'

'Quite likely,' Buck agreed. 'Say, if'n you bump into her, will yuh ask her if'n she's had that search yet, an' if'n it was successful? Mention us, an' she'll know what yuh mean.'

'Sure, I'll ask her, but I'm blessed if I know what you mean,' replied Smith. 'I'm afraid I've been too concerned about Johnny to pay much attention to what else is going on around here. Selfish of me, I suppose. I'm sorry.'

'Not at all, Mr. Smith. Obviously yo're worried about yore son. It's the only reason yo're out here, ain't it? You ain't got no cause to concern yoreself with any other business. Let us do the worryin' over that.' Buck pushed his plate away and began rolling a cigarette. 'Yo're payin' us to produce Johnny, but we can't do that until Dan Beardow's murderer is revealed. At the moment, the law wants yore son, and as soon as he shows up the sheriff will slap him in jail. As long as he stays outa jail, the killer is goin' to remain edgy. I'm hopin' he'll show his hand before too long. One slip on his part, and Johnny's a free man.'

He leaned back and lit up, watching Smith, who was staring thoughtfully at his empty plate.

'Well,' the older man said at length, 'I suppose you're right. But, what if Johnny did give himself up? Wouldn't that show he was innocent and that he had faith in the law? And wouldn't the real killer be likely to get a little careless then, thinking he was safe?'

It was Buck's turn to look pensive. 'Mebbe,' he admitted. 'But out here, Mr. Smith, the law ain't quite as thorough as it might be in Boston. There's many a man been hung on little or no evidence, an' the case closed. Sometimes it acts pretty quickly, too, an' yore Johnny might find hisself on the wrong end of a rope before the killer gets a mite careless, *sabe*?'

'Yes, I suppose you're right,' Smith concurred. 'What's your next move?'

'Well,' drawled Buck, taking a deep drag on his cigarette, 'since 'most everyone seems to have come to town, I guess we'll jist mingle a little an' keep our eyes an' ears open wide.'

Smith stood up. 'I wish you boys luck,' he said. 'I'm off to the store now.'

'So long, Mr. Smith. See yuh around.'

They watched Smith depart and then Zeke grinned at Buck. 'How's the haid now, pardner?'

'Good as new,' replied Buck.

'Good, 'cause I'm thinkin' mebbe you'll need it if'n the BE boys are in town along with everybody else. D'yuh think they'll have a stab at gettin' their own back on us?'

'I'll be ready for 'em, Zeke. Remember, Bull's no back-shooter, an' I can cope with whatever goes off in front of me.'

They walked out of the hotel and stood blinking in the sunlight, surveying the crowded main street. The burly

93

figure of Hank Rawlins was making its way towards them across the dusty street.

'Moose tells me you boys got yoreselves a piece o' evidence,' he said without preamble.

'We got ourselves a piece o' steer which appears to have swapped allegiance from the PF to the BE,' Buck confirmed. 'Want to see it?'

The sheriff stuck his hand out in answer and Buck handed him the hide. Hank examined the fragment carefully and then pocketed it himself.

'I'll keep this as exhibit 'A',' he told them. 'It's clear enough that that steer had its brand altered from PF to BE. D'you two want to come along with me and we'll confront Bram Ewell with it?'

'Any of that BE crowd will jist nat'rally deny all knowledge of it, Sheriff,' replied Buck. 'What are yuh goin' to do then? Arrest all of 'em on suspicion?'

'You think this ain't enough? Am I supposed to catch somebody actually alterin' the brands before they'll admit it?'

'All it proves is that rustlin' is takin' place, which we knew anyhow. We still don't know who's doin' it, do we?'

'If the brands are bein' changed to BE, then they are doin' it, ain't they?'

'Not necessarily. I figger that somebody wants to ruin the PF ranch, an' the best way to do that is to make sure that they never have enough cattle for another round-up. The fact that the BE stock is growin' at the PF's expense may be jist that it's so easy to alter PF to BE.'

Hank sniffed. 'I didn't know you was such an almighty big friend of the BE, mister. In fact, accordin' to reports you got a bunch of 'em sore at yuh the first day yuh hit town. Now yuh want me to ignore this evidence of rustlin' by 'em and jist let 'em carry on doin' it. Am I right?'

Buck grinned easily. 'Not exactly, Sheriff. When yuh got 'em dead to rights, then yuh can arrest the whole blamed outfit as far as I'm concerned. I think the murders are tied up in this somewheres, an' gettin' the rustlers ain't gonna help Johnny Smith, is it? He ain't accused of rustlin', jist a killin'.'

The sheriff pondered on that for a moment. Then he sighed heavily.

'I get yore point, cowboy,' he said. 'Murder is a more serious crime, an' if we're after the wrong man, an' I ain't sayin' we are, then there could be some more things to learn about both the killin' and the rustlin'.'

'Meanin' why Dan an' Pete was killed, an' why the cows are bein' stolen.'

'Hold on a minute,' said the sheriff sharply. 'Yuh mean Pete Farrow? Who said anythin' about him? That was years ago.'

'Yeah, an' no-one was ever accused of his murder,' said Buck. 'Somebody did it.'

'They could be in Montanny or Mexico by now.'

'I don't think so, Sheriff. I'm willin' to bet that the killer ain't a dozen miles from here right now.'

The sheriff frowned. 'Why should he hang around here?'

'We don't know his motive, do we? I suspect that he didn't completely achieve his objective with that murder, but he's still hopin'. No point in him leavin' with a job half done, is there?'

'I dunno what yo're drivin' at, cowboy, but I'm gonna trust yuh.' Hank's face broke into a grin. 'Mebbe I'm loco, but I've a feelin' you'll come up with somethin' pretty soon. I'm only a ridin', shootin' sheriff, I ain't got no brains to speak of, but I think yo're on the level.'

'He puzzles me sometimes, Sheriff,' put in Zeke. 'I think he suffers from them thar brains yuh spoke of. Mighty complicated things, brains. It's best not to encourage 'em too much, they only confuse yuh. If'n yuh leave 'em alone, they jist lie down an' nat'rally go to sleep.'

Hank chuckled and walked away, shaking his head.

Zeke filled his pipe and lit it. Then he looked at Buck quizzically.

'Yuh let him keep the evidence,' he accused. 'Was that wise?'

'He is the sheriff,' replied Buck.

Zeke puffed at his corncob, savouring the tobacco. 'Yeah, but if'n yuh turn all the evidence we get over to him, when the time comes for a showdown do we get paid?'

'Five dollars a day was the agreement, big fella.'

'I was countin' on a big bonus at the end, when the Smiths are overjoyed at their reunitin'.'

'Yore thinkin' is too mercenary,' Buck told him soberly. 'Think of the joy of the Smiths. The satisfaction of a job well done should be reward enough, even for a bum like you.'

'Yuh sound jist like a preacher I once knowed. Allus talkin' about gettin' yore reward in heaven, till he was caught helpin' to rob a bank. I guess he got his reward in jail, after all.'

Buck laughed. 'C'mon, let's take a

look around the town an' see who's here.'

They ambled down the sidewalk, to all appearances a couple of drifting cowboys without a care in the world.

'There's a lotta strangers in town,' commented Zeke.

'Yeah, an' some we've met before,' Buck said, pointing to a lean, rangy puncher across the street. Nat Cross saw them coming towards him, and hitched at his pants nervously. 'Hi, Nat,' called Buck. 'I see you've got yoreself a new hat.'

Nat touched his white sombrero self-consciously.

'Uh-huh. Cost me all of twelve dollars,' he declared.

'Is that so? Did the old one suffer from mothholes? Or was it a bullet-hole?'

The cowboy shot Buck a venomous glare and hurried into the Bald Eagle, seeking the safety of some of his BE companions.

Zeke laughed. 'Looks like yuh touched

on a sore spot there, Buck,' he said.

They strolled for a few yards and met Art Nelson and Bart Keene, two of the Bar L punchers. They stood talking to them for a few moments on range topics. Suddenly Bart let out a whoop.

'Will ya lookit that!' he exclaimed. 'Repeater's come round at last.'

From an alley at the side of the saloon emerged a dishevelled looking Repeater Riley, red-eyed and blinking furiously in the sunlight. They watched as he staggered over to a horse-trough and dunked his head in, and then came up gasping for air.

'Looks like he got the granddaddy of hang-overs,' chuckled Art. 'Fer an almost teetotal man, he shore sank a lot of whiskey last night.'

'I wonder if'n he can still stow away grub like he done yes'day?' Zeke pondered.

'Let's ask him if'n he fancies a nice big breakfast,' laughed Buck.

Before he could make a move towards Repeater, Bull Bartram rode up and accosted the wrangler.

'What you doin' here, Repeater?' he snarled. 'The boss's been lookin' all over fer yuh. There's some fences need fixin' on the western range.'

Bull's face was twisted with contempt and his jaw was swollen to twice its normal size, adding to his ugly look.

'Uh, sorry, Mr. Bartram. I, er — ' Repeater stammered.

'Yuh'll shore be in trouble, yuh no-good bum,' raged the BE ramrod, looking vainly for an empty hitching-rail.

'It ain't Repeater's fault, Bartram,' said Buck evenly. 'I brought him to town.'

Bull whirled in his saddle to face the voice. On seeing the four of them, his eyes widened and then narrowed into slits as he focused on Zeke. Hatred welled up in him, but he was not fool enough to make any play.

'Which one of you jackasses said that?' he spat.

'I did,' replied Buck. 'Can't a feller

101

treat his buddy to a meal an' a drink once in a while without you shovin' yore ugly puss in?'

Seething at the insult, Bull swallowed involuntarily. If the odds had been less than four to one, he would probably have reached for his guns. As it was, he controlled himself with an effort and pointed at the sorry-looking Repeater.

'Look at the state he's in,' he fumed. 'He won't be fit for hours yet. I'm holdin' you responsible, cowboy.'

'You are, huh?' Buck said easily. 'An' what do yuh propose to do about it?'

'I — I'll thrash him till he larns some sense, that's what.'

'Jist a minute,' went on Buck. 'Yuh jist held me responsible, remember? Why don't yuh try thrashin' me?'

Bull grinned humourlessly. 'An' have yore pet gorilla tear me in half? I ain't that stupid. This drunken fool belongs to the BE, an' I do the punishin' fer that outfit, *sabe*?'

'You lay a finger on my pal there an' you'll collect a hole in yore vest,' Buck threatened coldly.

For an instant the BE foreman's hands hovered over his guns, but he caught the deadly look in Buck's eyes and knew that his adversary meant what he said. The lean cowpuncher unnerved him and he returned his attention to Repeater.

'You get on back to the ranch, pronto,' he ordered. 'The boss'll deal with yuh.' Then without a glance at the crowd which had gathered, he spurred his horse and galloped down the street.

Repeater looked appealingly at Buck.

'My hoss,' he groaned. 'I gotta find my hoss. Where'd I leave it, Mr. Lawrence?'

'I expect Ed stabled it back o' the saloon,' Buck suggested kindly. 'Let's go find it, Repeater.'

He led the forlorn figure to the stables and helped him mount his little pinto.

'You get back to the ranch now an' don't worry about that big bully, yuh hear?' he told Repeater.

'What'll he do to me, Mr. Lawrence?' whimpered Repeater. 'Will he fire me, huh? Fire me.'

'No, he's only the foreman, an' I think he's more worried about what I'll do to him,' replied Buck. 'You go an' report to yore boss. Tell him yuh went to town with the boys an' decided to stay overnight. It's the truth, ain't it?'

'Yeah, it's true. That's right, tell the truth.'

'If'n that Bartram threatens yuh, you jist remind him he's liable to become separated from his hide if'n he touches yuh. Got that?'

'Yeah, I got it. Thanks, Mr. Lawrence. Nobody ever looked after me before. I feel better already. Better already.'

Buck grinned and gave the pinto a friendly whack on its rump.

'So long, pal, be seein' yuh!' he called as horse and rider raced away into the main street.

6

After a couple of drinks in the Bald Eagle, the two ex-punchers arranged to meet in the hotel at dinner, Buck riding out to find a quiet spot in the hills to practise fast draws and target-shooting. Zeke ambled along to the hotel.

He had reached the foot of the stairs when a shout stopped him.

'Hey, Mr. Henderson.' It was Pete McCall, the receptionist, his watery eyes blinking at the giant figure across the shadowy reception hall. 'Nearly missed yuh. One o' them BE fellers came in earlier an' brought somethin' for yore pardner. Said he'd left it over at the ranch after payin' a visit. I let him take it up to yore room, hope that's awright. He was only there fer a minute.'

Zeke frowned. 'Which BE feller was that, Pete?'

'A fat, flabby — '

'Lem Ritchie!'

'That's the one. He had somethin' in a sack.'

Zeke grunted. 'I'm shore bettin' he ain't playin' Santy Claus.'

He hurried up to the bedroom, his mind turning over the possibilities of this latest move by the BE. Neither he nor Buck had ever been near the BE ranch, and whatever Lem had been to their room for he was certain the flabby puncher was up to no good. The thought occurred to him that Ritchie no doubt expected that they would not return until it was time to go to bed, by which time the receptionist would have gone off duty and could not have given them any warning.

Reaching the door, Zeke opened it cautiously and looked carefully around. Everything appeared to be exactly as they had left it. He examined both his and Buck's warbags, but nothing was missing. Sitting on the edge of his bed, he pulled off his boots and sat quietly, thinking. His eyes roamed the room;

there was nothing, no sign of the BE man's visit.

Strange, he thought. Lem had not gone through the rigmarole with the receptionist just to view the decorations. No doubt he had kept observation on Buck and himself until they had entered the saloon, and then he would have made his move.

Suddenly, he was aware of something. Above the street noises outside he heard nothing, and yet there seemed to be *something*. It was not a sound, but more a movement. His scalp prickled and he rubbed his tongue round his dry mouth. Leaping from the bed, he turned and grabbed a spare curtain rod, propped against the wall in the corner of the room.

He could still see nothing, but a faint, almost imperceptible movement in the bedclothes caught his eye. With the brass rod raised in his right hand, he carefully grasped the corner of the blanket and jerked it back.

There, regarding him with a steady,

deadly gaze, lay a sidewinder. Upon exposure, it immediately curled itself in the position which gives the snake its name, and prepared to strike. Zeke crashed the curtain rod on the snake's head, and repeated the operation until he was sure the noxious reptile was dead. Then, with a grimace, he lifted it on the rod and dropped it out of the window. Few things scared the huge cowpuncher, but snakes always sent shudders of fear through his giant frame.

He sat down again and breathed deeply, letting his heartbeat gradually return to normal. Then, after another careful search of the room and an even more careful scrutiny of Buck's bed, he lay down and began to think.

If he had come in late at night, undressed and got into bed the snake would have struck repeatedly before he had gathered his wits. A shiver ran through him as he contemplated his probable fate. It reminded him of his first meeting with the man who was to become his inseparable partner.

Zeke had been heading west from Texas, reached the Rio Grande and then struck north. Buck had come in the opposite direction from Arizona and also turned north at the river.

After the usual Western greetings and banter they had struck up an immediate attachment to each other and rode together for a few miles. As they passed a clump of bushes, Zeke's horse suddenly reared, unseating its rider. He was flung into a bush and lay momentarily dazed. From less than a foot from his face came a warning rattle, and he opened his eyes to see a deadly diamond-back poised to strike. Another second and the rattlesnake's fangs would have injected their venom into him, but Buck's Colt roared and shattered the reptile's head.

Zeke thought then that he would always be in the green-eyed puncher's debt, but fate decreed that he pay it back that very same day. Arriving in a small desert town at about dusk, they had entered the only saloon to slake their thirsts and Buck had got into a poker game with a local tinhorn. Buck had accused the gambler of cheating and while the argument raged, Zeke, who was watching from the side of the table, saw the gambler draw his gun and prepare to shoot underneath the table. Zeke's fingertips were gripping the table and he tipped it violently, knocking the weapon away. The big puncher had then given the treacherous tinhorn a lesson in manners which he would never forget.

Since that day, the two had become constant companions, sharing many jobs and many adventures. Chuckling to himself as he recalled some of the incidents, Zeke gradually drifted off into sleep.

* * *

He awoke after several hours and went downstairs to dinner to find Buck and Frank Smith already at the table.

110

'Howdy, Lazybones,' greeted his partner, 'had a good sleep? Yuh know, Mr. Smith, it's jist plumb nat'ral that Zeke allus wakes up when it's time to eat. He's more reliable than the best alarm clock.'

Zeke ignored the sarcasm and told them about Lem's visit and the surprise he had left in the bed.

Buck looked serious and said, 'Looks like we gotta be prepared for attacks from all angles. They shore must be scared of us, though. Even if the snake had bitten yuh, McCall would have told about Ritchie's visit at the inquest.'

'That's a comfortin' thought,' snorted Zeke.

They finished the meal and all three produced the makings, Zeke filling his corncob, Buck rolling a quirly and Smith taking a little gadget from his pocket and setting it on the table.

'What the divil is that?' queried Zeke.

Smith grinned and placed a cigarette paper in the rollers and sprinkled tobacco over it.

'I ran out of cigarettes and I discovered when I tried to roll some that I was all thumbs and spilt most of the tobacco,' he said, turning a little wheel at the side of the machine. 'I was surprised when I found that the local store stocked these. They're common out East, you know.'

Moments later he produced a perfectly rolled cigarette and lit it with a flourish.

'Well, I'll be darned!' exclaimed Zeke. 'What will they think of next?'

'By the way,' said Smith, 'I saw Alice and gave her your message. She said no, she hadn't found it yet, but she'd keep on looking. She's invited me over to the PF ranch for dinner tomorrow.'

'Good fer you,' declared Buck. 'She shore is a fine woman.'

'She certainly is,' agreed Smith.

'You know, Buck, I been thinkin',' said Zeke slowly.

'That shore musta strained yore intellect,' Buck replied. 'Mebbe if'n yuh go an' lie down agin it'll pass off.'

'The bartender at the saloon said them BE boys ain't never missed a Sat'day night, didn't he?' Zeke mused.

'Yeah, that's right,' admitted Buck. 'You thinkin' of goin' across an' apologisin' to Lem for killin' his snake?'

'Not exactly, but don'tcha think the BE crowd will think they got us scared, if'n we don't show up?'

'So what? I ain't a carin' what them coyotes think, one way or another. Besides, I think I'd better ease off on the likker fer a while.'

'Well, I ain't thinkin' no such thing an' I reckon a couple of beers won't disable me none.'

Buck ground out his cigarette in an ashtray. 'If'n yo're thinkin' of lookin' fer Lem Ritchie, you'll be wastin' yore time. He won't come near Peaceful till he hears yo're six feet under.'

'That's where yo're wrong, lean feller. He ain't expectin' us to discover that sidewinder till tonight. He'll be celebratin' an' boastin' to his cronies about it.'

Buck looked at the giant in admiration. 'By gosh! Yo're right, Zeke. It ain't all muscle up there between yore ears.'

'So mebbe yuh could risk a sarsaparilla an' observe the fun,' suggested Zeke.

'In case the rest of 'em gang up on yuh?'

'It would only be the BE crowd. The decent citizens would love to see him discomforted.'

'It sounds like this Ritchie isn't the most popular man in Peaceful,' observed Smith.

'He's so unpopular,' said Buck, 'even his own shadder won't foller him.'

Smith laughed and stood up.

'Well, boys,' he said. 'I've got some correspondence to write. Be careful, I don't want to pay out funeral expenses on top of my five dollars a day.'

'We can take care of ourselves, Mr. Smith,' Buck assured him as they parted.

The hotel boasted a wooden porch overlooking the sidewalk and Buck and

Zeke ensconced themselves in a couple of rocking-chairs. Buck manufactured a fresh cigarette and Zeke methodically filled his pipe. They sat there, apparently at peace with the world, but their eyes took in every movement on the street.

Punchers were riding or strolling up to the Bald Eagle at the rate of about one every minute, and soon the sounds of laughter and raucous voices began drifting from the saloon. Hank Rawlins and Moose Roberts left the sheriff's office and ambled over towards the saloon.

Hank paused as he reached the two cowpunchers and nodded.

'I been thinkin' about what yuh said about Pete Farrow,' he said. 'You shore you boys don't know somethin' I should?'

'We don't actually know anythin', Sheriff,' said Buck. 'Jist suspect. We might also find out what happened to Lije Guthrie, it all depends on our informant. It might take a little time, he's a little reluctant to say much. Soon as we git anythin' definite, we'll let yuh know.'

The sheriff nodded again, and he and Moose went into the saloon.

Chuck Wiseman was next to arrive. As he tied his horse to the hitching-rail, he called, 'Howdy, boys. Comin' over for a game of penny-ante? Won't cost yuh more than a month's wages.'

'Mebbe later, Chuck,' replied Zeke. 'We're jist gettin' a little evenin' air. It's been powerful hot today.'

'Shore has,' agreed Chuck. 'An' I've worked up a thirst to match.'

After another ten minutes, in which time several more punchers had entered the Bald Eagle, Zeke spotted his quarry. Riding slowly, engaged in animated conversation, came Lem Ritchie and Nat Cross. Lem was wearing a dirty bandage fixed roughly round his head. He was also wearing a pleased expression on his fat face. They failed to notice the two men on the porch in the gathering gloom, and pulled up at the saloon.

Zeke was half-way across the street when they turned at the sound of his spurs jingling.

'What's the idea, Ritchie, puttin' one o' yore relatives in my bed?' demanded Zeke coldly.

Both men dropped their hands to their guns, but Buck spoke from the darkened porch.

'Jist keep yore mitts away from them pistols, gents,' he warned. ''Less'n yuh require ventilatin'.'

'I dunno what yo're talkin' about,' blurted Ritchie, withdrawing his hands.

'Yuh don't, huh? Mebbe this'll refresh yore memory.' Zeke strode up to him, seized him by the scruff of the neck and the seat of his overalls, lifted him bodily into the air and marched over to a horse trough outside the livery stable. Then he dunked the hapless puncher in the water and held him there.

'Hey, stop it, yuh'll drown him,' protested Nat.

Zeke hauled Lem out and the

BE man gasped and spluttered and struggled helplessly in the giant's grip.

'No, he ain't drownin',' Zeke informed Nat. 'I think he's shoutin' for more. Mebbe he's a watersnake instead of a sidewinder.'

He dumped the unfortunate Lem under again and then released his hold. Lem surfaced, choked in some air, and scrambled out of the trough.

'Guess he never did like water,' commented Buck, laughing. 'Either for drinkin' or washin'.'

Lem leaned on the side of the trough, taking in great gulps of air, water cascading from his hat, miraculously still jammed on his head.

'Say, who's the human waterfall?' called a voice.

All except Lem, who had other things on his mind, turned to see the lean figure of Duke Summerville dismounting outside the saloon.

'Howdy, Duke,' greeted Zeke. 'We figgered Lem here was needin' a bath, so I jist obliged.'

'Well, there don't seem to be no towels around to dry him,' Duke observed. 'Nat, you'd better take yore pardner home an' change him afore he gits pneumony.'

'Mebbe snakes don't git pneumony,' suggested Buck. 'But I guess he is more used to gettin' wet inside, 'stead of outside.'

Nat tried to put a consoling arm around the saturated puncher, who shrugged him away and snarled, 'Lemme be, I don't need no damn nurse. I can change my own clothes.'

Duke chuckled. 'He don't need no wet nurse, he means, Nat. He's wet enough as it is.'

The BE men remounted and rode away. Zeke explained to Duke about the sidewinder in his bed and the Bar L ramrod's jaw hardened.

'If'n I'd a' knowed that, I'd a' dumped him in that trough myself, an' mebbe not so gently,' he said grimly. 'C'mon, lemme buy yuh a drink.'

Zeke said he could use a beer after

the excitement and Buck somewhat shamefully agreed to a sarsaparilla.

★　★　★

Frank Smith breakfasted alone the next day, Buck and Zeke sleeping late behind the barricaded door to their room. Smith had purchased the best items of jewellery in the general store, a matching necklace and brooch, which he had carefully wrapped up as a present for Alice.

After breakfast, he went across to the livery stable and hired a gentle-looking roan and set off for the PF ranch. His heart was light as he rode through the cottonwoods to the north-east of town, climbed the hill and reached the vast, open rangeland at the top. He was beginning to love this wild, rough country with its everlasting vistas and rugged scenery, despite the presence of some unsavoury characters and the ever-present threat of violence they presented. A great many of the inhabitants of Peaceful were honest and reliable, if tough, folk. He still had a nagging anxiety about the safety of his son, but he trusted the two cowpunchers he had hired. He liked their quaint language and humour and felt sure they would soon unmask the killer of Dan Beardow, who perhaps had also murdered Alice's husband.

Then, when the trouble was all cleared up, what would he do? His life, up to last week, had consisted of Smith's Pickles in Boston, but now, somehow, all that seemed so very long ago as well as far away. Maybe, like Johnny, he had some of the blood of the Westerner in his veins. The thought made him chuckle as he urged the little roan into a canter.

About half-way to the ranch he spotted three horsemen in the distance. He adjusted his glasses, but his eyes were not accustomed to the great distances of the plains and he could not make out who they were. They had obviously spotted him, for one was pointing in his direction. They appeared to have a somewhat heated discussion and then he saw them start to ride towards him.

What should he do? he wondered. It was no use trying to outrun them; an inexperienced horseman on the little roan would not stand a chance in a race with three cowboys used to a lifetime in the saddle. But, maybe he was worrying for nothing. No-one could possibly want to interfere with an inoffensive tenderfoot. Probably it was normal custom to ride up and greet a stranger out on the range. Then he remembered the necklace and brooch and realised that he could be worth robbing.

By this time, however, the riders had covered a great deal of the distance between them and him, and it was too late to flee. As they drew near he realised with horror that they were all wearing bandannas over their noses and he could see only six eyes peering at him beneath wide-brimmed hats.

The owner of two of the eyes, a large,

bulky individual, growled at him, the voice muffled by the dirty red neckerchief covering his face.

'Yo're Johnny Smith's dad, ain't yuh?'

'Why — er — yes, I am,' stammered Smith. It was no use denying it, they knew very well who he was.

'Yo're comin' with us,' ordered the man, producing a formidable looking Colt. 'Git his eyes covered, boys, this is gonna be a mystery trip fer Mr. Smith.'

'Why are you doing this?' demanded Smith. 'Where are you taking me?'

'Shut yore mouth, or I'll slug yuh!' retorted the masked man.

Smith had the presence of mind to pocket his glasses as one of the other bandits bandaged his eyes. Then he felt his horse being led away. He could feel the sun on his back and calculated they were taking him in a north-westerly direction.

How would anyone ever find him in this vast wilderness? he wondered. Then he remembered something and a glimmer of hope entered his mind. Casually, as if shifting position for comfort, he let his hand slide into his pocket, hoping desperately that none of the men were watching.

7

Alice Farrow was busy in the kitchen when she heard hoofbeats outside. Hurrying to the door, her heart sank when she opened it and saw Bram Ewell dismounting. She had been expecting Frank Smith and the troublesome rancher was the last person she wished to see.

'Hello, Alice,' said Ewell, striding up to the door. He sniffed appreciatively. 'My, that cookin' shore smells good. Mind if I have a word with you? You ain't got company, have you?'

'No, but I'm expecting someone at any moment,' she replied. 'It's rather inconvenient — '

'Shucks, I won't take up much of yore time. Lemme come in an' set a spell. I'll leave when yore visitors arrive.'

Reluctantly, she admitted him. Tossing his hat carelessly on to a chair, he sprawled himself on the sofa, lit a stogie, and blew a cloud of smoke at the ceiling.

'What was it you wished to see me about, Mr. Ewell?' Alice asked. She did not sit down.

'Call me Bram, Alice,' Ewell returned. 'I guess we know each other well enough to be on first-name terms.'

Alice did not reply, so Ewell continued. 'I'll come straight to the point. As it is now, yore ranch is finished. You've got no hands an' yuh can't possibly run this place on yore own. Sooner or later you'll have to get out. I've got an alternative suggestion.'

'When Johnny comes back, we'll get something organised,' Alice said hotly. 'And I don't see what business it is of yours, Mr. Ewell.'

Ewell laughed shortly. 'That murderer won't be back. If he shows up in this valley the sheriff will have him in jail an' he'll finish up on the end of a rope.'

'Not if there's any justice, he won't. A lot of people think he's innocent.'

Ewell ignored her protestation. 'I've allus thought a lot of yuh, Alice,' he went on. 'If'n you'll marry me, we can join the two ranches an' you'll keep yore share in the biggest spread in this valley. Yuh need a man to protect yuh from rustlers an' all the dangers of this country.'

'No, Mr. Ewell,' said Alice firmly. 'For one thing, I don't love you, and I'm quite capable of looking after myself.'

'You jist consider what I'm offerin'. A life of wealth an' ease — the alternative is a hopeless struggle which'll leave yuh broke an' miserable.'

'I'll take the alternative,' Alice said coldly. 'Now if you've said your piece, will you please leave and let me get on with my work?'

Ewell's eyes narrowed and his lips curled into a snarl. 'Have it yore own way, then. But don't say I didn't warn yuh, I'll finish up with this ranch, one way or another.'

He snatched up his hat and stormed out. Alice watched him mount his horse and gallop away. Then she sank into a chair and buried her face in her hands. She made no attempt to stop the flow of tears.

★   ★   ★

It was well into the afternoon before Luke Simms rounded up all his passengers for the return trip to Brent Creek. He was leading the last stragglers away from the Bald Eagle towards the battered old Concord, when his eyes alighted on a new notice pinned to the board outside the sheriff's office. He stared open-mouthed at the missive, read it twice, and then tore it down.

'Shan't be a minute, boys,' he announced to the confused passengers. 'I gotta give this to the sheriff *pronto*. You jist git yoreselves settled comfortably on the stage.'

Rushing back into the saloon, Luke pushed his way through the crowd of cowboys and located Hank and Moose, who were engrossed in conversation

with Buck, Zeke and Ed, the bartender.

'Sheriff,' he panted, waving the sheet
of paper, 'you got this pinned to yore
notice-board. Have yuh read it?'

'If'n I pinned it there, then I've read
it, yuh bow-legged leprechaun,' replied
the sheriff.

'Don't be so darned disrespectful,'
snorted Luke. 'Ten bucks says you ain't
read this, or we'd all a'heard about it.'

'Lemme see that paper,' retorted
Hank, snatching it from Luke's hand.

Hank's eyebrows lifted as he started
to read and kept on rising until they
threatened to disappear under his
stetson.

'What's it say, Hank?' asked Ed,
craning his neck over the bar.

His eyebrows now having lowered
into a frown, Hank handed the paper to
the bartender.

'Read it out loud, Ed,' invited Art
Nelson. 'It'll take all day if'n we keep
handin' it round.'

'It says,' began Ed, ' 'We got Frank

Smith. If his murderin' son wants him to live he'd better surrender to the sheriff *pronto*.' It's signed 'Well-wishers'.'

'Wellwishers my foot!' exclaimed Duke Summerville. 'That's kidnappin'!'

'That poor ol' feller ain't been here long enough to git a suntan,' growled Art. 'He ain't done nothin' to nobody.'

'It'll give him a poor opinion of Western hospitality,' put in Buck. 'An' he was payin' our wages, too.'

'Yeah, that's right,' agreed Zeke. 'We gotta get him back or we get nothin'.'

'We'll git a posse organised right away,' suggested Art. 'How about it, Hank?'

'All right,' said the sheriff. 'But where do we start lookin'?'

'Frank Smith said he was ridin' over to the PF today,' Buck told him. 'My guess is he was interrupted in his journey there.'

'There should be fresh tracks to show whereabouts,' contributed Chuck Wiseman. 'Mebbe there was a scuffle.'

'Right, boys,' said the sheriff. 'Let's go!'

Duke was first to the door, but paused as he opened it.

'Oh, no!' he groaned. 'Will yuh lookit that!'

An incessant roar swept into the saloon from the open door. Outside it was as black as night and the road was a sea of mud.

'Any tracks they may have left will be gone by now,' Chuck pointed out. 'What a time fer it to rain!'

'Mebbe it's jist a local storm,' suggested Art. 'What's it look like over towards the PF?'

Hank stepped out into the street and lowered his stetson to keep the rain from his eyes.

'Blacker 'n ever that way, boys,' he announced gloomily. 'Shucks, I reckon it'll be futile lookin' now. Yuh'd have a hell of a time findin' the ranch in this, never mind a few tracks.'

They walked disconsolately back to the bar.

★ ★ ★

Duke Summerville carried the news to Bill Langham later that evening. After the cowhands had eaten supper and retired to the bunkhouse, Langham sought out Johnny Smith.

When Johnny saw Langham's grim face he realised that he was the bearer of bad tidings.

'What is it, Bill?' he asked anxiously. 'Somethin's happened, ain't it?'

'I'm afraid it's bad news, Johnny,' Langham told him. His normally humorous face was creased with worry. 'They got yore pa.'

'Got Pa? Who has?'

Langham explained about the note pinned to the sheriff's notice board.

Thoroughly alarmed, Johnny paced the room wildly.

'It don't make sense,' he maintained. 'No decent citizens would do a thing like that to an old man. It must be the killers themselves, an' they know blamed well I didn't murder Dan.'

132

'Now, calm down a bit, Johnny,' Langham soothed. 'We gotta figger this thing out. It looks to me that they want you outa the way. They won't feel safe until they've got yuh behind bars.'

Johnny was strapping on his gunbelt.

'I'll git those murderin' kidnappers,' he growled. 'They must have Pa somewheres around here. I'll find him if'n I have to search every inch o' these ranges.'

Langham put a hand on Johnny's shoulder.

'That's no good, son,' he said quietly. 'Remember, they're killers. If they get the slightest hint that yo're searchin' for him, they're quite likely to shoot yore pa an' leave yuh to find a corpse. It ain't a ransom they're after, yuh know. If they git the chance, they'll shoot you, too.'

'What can I do then, Bill?'

'Only thing is to turn yoreself in to the sheriff. Hank Rawlins is a fair man, even if he ain't so bright. He'll keep yuh safe until them two boys yore pa hired find the real killer.'

'You don't think they'll stop lookin' now that Pa's been captured?'

'All the more reason fer 'em to double their efforts. They don't get no pay until yore pa's back, do they? I only met one of 'em once, but I'd trust 'em.'

'Yeah, I know what yuh mean. That Zeke's as straight as a die.'

'Then you'll do it?'

Kate walked into the room and caught the last question.

'Do what, Dad?'

The men turned and regarded her apprehensively.

'Something's come up,' Langham said laconically. 'Johnny's leaving.'

'Why, what's happened?' Her eyes grew big and questioning.

Johnny stepped over to her and took her in his arms.

'I'm goin' to give myself up, Kate,' he said. When he saw the look in her eyes, he went on. 'No, not because I've done anything wrong. They've got my father, an' they'll kill him if I don't. I've got no choice.'

'Who's got your father? Will somebody please explain — '

Langham repeated the story for her, and when he had finished Kate sobbed on his shoulder.

'It's all for the best, Kate,' her father said, patting her blonde head. 'Johnny couldn't stay hidin' here for ever.'

'Will yuh come an' visit me, Kate?' Johnny asked with an attempt at a grin.

'Of course, Johnny,' she replied, wiping a tear away. 'Every day.'

'Better take a slicker if yo're goin' now,' advised Langham. 'And take it easy when you reach our eastern boundary — there's some pretty rough country out there an' it's been rainin' for five or six hours. Some o' them slopes can be treacherous if yore hoss puts a foot wrong.'

'I'll be careful, Bill,' Johnny assured him. 'I ain't in such a hurry to get to jail that I'll break a leg doin' it.'

★   ★   ★

At first Hank Rawlins thought the incessant pounding was all in his head. He had partaken quite a bit more than his usual quota of Ed's liquor and it had been close on midnight when he and Moose had finally quit the premises and staggered the few yards through the pouring rain to the sheriff's office. It seemed to him that he had only just laid his head down when the violent hammering began. Gradually he realised that most of it was reaching him through his ears, and that the noise was being caused by someone battering at the door and not inside his skull.

Wearily he groped around, found some matches, struck one and located the clock. The time showed a few minutes off two o'clock.

'What the hell's goin' on?' he muttered to himself, climbing out of the bed and lurching across to the window. Flinging it wide open, he thrust his head out, heedless of the rain, and peered into the gloomy night.

'Who is it?' he yelled into the

blackness. 'What do you want at this time o' night, disturbin' the peace an' — '

'I'm Johnny Smith,' a voice called from below. 'I've come to give myself up.'

'Johnny — ?' Realisation sobered up the sheriff immediately. His fumbling fingers found the matches again and lit an oil lamp by the bedside. Without pausing to cover up his night attire, he made his way down the stairs and unbolted the front door.

The rain-soaked figure stepped inside and Hank blinked at him owlishly.

'Yuh picked a fine time to give yoreself up,' he said disgustedly.

'I only just heard about my pa bein' kidnapped,' explained Johnny.

'Where have yuh been hidin' yoreself since Dan was killed?'

'That don't matter now I'm here, does it?'

'No, I suppose not,' grumbled the sheriff. 'I must say I'm surprised. I never thought you was a killer, Johnny.'

'I'm not, me an' Dan were pals,' protested the cowboy, climbing out of his wet slicker. 'But I can't let them harm my pa, so here I am.'

'All right, I'll lock yuh in the cell. Have yuh had any supper?'

'Yes, I've eaten.'

'That's a relief, yuh won't want feedin' till mornin' then. Better gimme yore gun.'

Johnny handed over his revolver and walked into the cell.

'We'll talk in the mornin',' said Hank, as he locked the door. 'An' see if yore version of what happened agrees with the Widder Farrow's. If not, then yo're in big trouble, son.'

★ ★ ★

Buck and Zeke were eating breakfast when the sheriff walked in and came over to them.

'Mornin', boys,' he greeted. 'I jist came to give yuh the news before I leave.'

138

Buck took a sip of his coffee and wiped his mouth with the back of his hand. 'What news is that, Hank, an' where are yuh goin'?'

The sheriff pulled up a vacant chair, straddled it, and rested his elbows on the back.

'Johnny Smith gave hisself up last night. Or rather, early this mornin',' he corrected.

'He did, huh? Musta heard about his pa bein' kidnapped.'

'That's right. So now I can do what I've been meanin' to do for some time — go over to Houston an' straighten things out with Dan Beardow's family.'

'That's an awful long ride, Sheriff,' put in Zeke.

'I'm only ridin' as far as the railroad,' explained Hank. 'The train'll get me there tomorrow. I'll be gone two, mebbe three, days, thassall. Moose can take care o' things at this end.'

Buck finished off the last mouthful and started rolling a cigarette.

'Meanwhile, the real killer and the

rustlers are still at large,' he said.

Hank sighed. 'Yeah, I know things ain't been straightened out yet. Mebbe a few days away'll help me sort a few things out in my mind. What are you boys doin' while I'm away?'

'I'm ridin' over to see the widder today,' replied Buck. 'Zeke here spent some time with the Navaho when he was young, an' they taught him trackin'. He'll be tryin' to find where they're keepin' Johnny's pa.'

'They'll be releasin' him now, won't they?'

Buck snorted. 'The note said he'd live, thassall. If'n they release him, he'll be able to tell where he's been, won't he? An' probably who captured him. Yuh don't think they'll want to give the game away that easy, do yuh? No, sir! I'll bet they keep on debatin' his fate for a long time.'

'Until the U.S. Marshal comes to take Johnny to the County Seat?'

'Or until Johnny swings for a crime he didn't commit.'

140

The sheriff was silent for a few minutes while Buck and Zeke lit up. 'Shore looks like I'm runnin' away from trouble, don't it?' he said sadly.

'Now, don't you fret none, Hank,' Zeke advised. 'Me an' Buck ain't been licked on a case yet. Buck's got more brains than the rest of us put together; he'll come up with somethin'. You jist go an' see Dan's fambly an' leave the dee-tectin' to us.'

'Well, thanks, boys,' said the sheriff humbly. 'It's nice to know I'm leavin' the town in such capable hands.'

After the sheriff had left, Buck looked quizzically at Zeke and said, 'Yo're goin' it a bit strong, Zeke, ain't yuh? Ain't never been licked on a case yet?'

Zeke grinned. 'It's true, Buck. Since this is our first case as dee-tectives, we ain't licked yet.'

* * *

The rain had stopped, but the sky was still overcast when the two self-styled detectives saddled their horses and set off down the street, which had been transformed overnight into a sea of mud.

'It's shore gonna be difficult findin' any tracks in this,' declared Zeke, looking disgustedly at the ground.

'We'll foller the usual trail to the PF,' said Buck. 'Smith must have gone that way. Mebbe there'll be some clue along the trail.'

The slope up to the open range was slippery and it took all the skill of horse and rider to keep their footing. They made it eventually, after much slipping and sliding, without becoming dislodged from their mounts. From there on the going was much easier and they were able to concentrate on studying the ground for any signs which had not been washed away by the heavy rain.

They were half-way to the ranch when Zeke, riding on the left, pulled his mount to a halt.

Buck reined too, and shot a searching glance at his partner. 'What is it, Zeke?

Seen somethin'?'

Zeke pointed to a spot some ten yards to the left where the sodden grass had been cropped short by feeding cattle.

'That ain't no stone,' Zeke declared. 'No natural object has a shape like that.'

Dismounting, he strode over and picked up the dull, metal thing, which stood out like a sore thumb to his trained eyes.

'Hey, look what we got here,' he called, and walked back to Buck, who took the object from him and examined it.

'Well, I'll be durned!' Buck exclaimed. 'Smith's cigareet-makin' machine!'

'Yeah, an' look, there's a whole lotta churned mud around here. This must be the place where he was kidnapped. See all that flattened grass leadin' over there — that must be where they took him.'

'Yo're right, Zeke. I'm thinkin' this is where we split up. Yo're a much better tracker than I am, you foller the trail as far as yuh can, an' I'll go on to the widder's. One of us should find out somethin' today.'

Pocketing the cigarette-maker, Buck urged his horse into a gallop, no longer needing to scrutinise the trail. Zeke went more carefully, following the newer and fainter trail to the north-west. After about a mile he lost the trail, had to backtrack for a while, and then found it again. He lost it several more times, but his Navaho training proved adequate in the end. Nevertheless, it took him over two hours to cover about six miles where, topping a rise, he saw smoke to the north. Making his way cautiously towards the fire, he was vastly relieved to recognise the lean figure of Repeater Riley intently watching a frying pan.

Repeater's vacant features registered no emotion as Zeke rode up to him.

'That shore smells good, Repeater,' said the giant, as he dropped the reins and dismounted nimbly.

Gradually an inane grin spread across

144

Repeater's countenance as he recognised Zeke.

'Uh, yo're Mr. Lawrence's friend, ain't yuh?' he said. 'Er — I — Mr. Lawrence's friend.'

'Zeke,' supplied the other. 'Yeah, that's right. How's the coffee?'

'Cawfee's fine, Zeke. Gen-yew-ine Arbuckle's. Got some bacon an' beans, if'n yuh want some. Got some jerky, too.'

'I'll settle for the bacon an' beans,' said Zeke, sitting on a flat boulder.

While they ate, Repeater chatted about his work and how they looked after him at the BE. Zeke allowed him to ramble on, finished his meal, and sipped his coffee.

'I guess you know this country pretty well, Repeater,' said Zeke at length. He realised it would be hard work, but he decided to try to get some information from the simple-minded wrangler.

'Yes, sir, pretty well. Knowed it ever since I can remember.'

'Are there any hidin' places around

here, Repeater? You know, cabins, an' the like.'

'Naw, not many.' Repeater racked his meagre brains. 'I know one, though, a line cabin in Greasewood Canyon, four, mebbe five miles over there.' He pointed in the direction Zeke had been heading.

'Anybody ever go there?'

'Mm. Couple crazy Mexicans hang out there sometimes. Mr. Ewell sometimes hires 'em. Sometimes hires drifters at round-up time, too. Crazy Mexicans.'

'These Mexicans, are they likely to be there now?'

'Dunno, Zeke. Ain't see'd 'em fer quite a spell. You lookin' fer 'em?'

'I'm lookin' for somebody, but I don't know if'n it's them or not.'

Repeater's face crinkled in puzzlement. 'I don't unnerstand that. Yo're lookin' fer somebody, but don't know who? Well, yuh found me, ain't I somebody?'

Zeke grinned. 'Shore yuh are,

Repeater. Yo're a good friend. An'a fine cook, too.'

Repeater beamed. 'Thanks, Mr — er — Zeke. I can cook yuh some more beans if'n yuh like. More beans.'

'No, thanks, I gotta be on my way. Yuh shore been a help to me. Say, yuh ain't seen a stranger out this way dressed in eastern clothes, have yuh?'

'No, Zeke, not a-tall. Never see'd no Easterner.' It was Repeater's turn to frown in perplexity again. 'What do they look like?'

'Sorta different. Never mind, Repeater. So long, I'll be seein' yuh.'

'So long. I shore hope so, it's nice havin' someone to talk to. Gits kinda lonely out here. Kinda lonely.'

Mumbling softly to himself, Repeater started tidying up, having forgotten Zeke's visit already.

8

'*Qué tal tiempo hace?*'

Lying on his back on the couch, his head cradled in both hands, Pedro Moreno opened his eyes as his brother flung the door open and gazed outside.

Miguel whirled and glared at the recumbent figure.

''Ow many times I tell you?' he snapped. 'Spik Eenglish in these America.'

'Sorry, *mi hermano*, I forget. The weather ees stop raining, no?'

'That better! *Si*, ees stop now.' For reasons known only to himself, Miguel always insisted that they practise their own peculiar brand of English while north of the border, even when speaking to each other. Pedro had begun to suspect that it was obligatory in the United States and if, as was his wont, he lapsed into his native Spanish for too long, then something dreadful would happen to them.

'I theenk I go see Maria,' went on Miguel. 'I'm fed ops in thees cabin for whole day.'

'W'at about heem?' Pedro asked, indicating Frank Smith, who sat on a chair in the corner of the room, hands bound behind him.

'You look after heem, eh? I go only from t'ree, four hours.'

'No! Eef you go to Brent Crik, I go, too. I gots friends there, we go for dreenks.'

'Eef those *vaqueros* find out we leave heem they weel be *furioso*. Mebbe they weel keel us. Besides you gots bottle *tequila* here, eef you wants dreenk.'

Pedro shook his head vehemently. 'Ees not the same. Mebbe I gets dronk, but eet ees better wit' my *amigos*.'

'You gots heem,' suggested Miguel. 'Mebbe you gets dronk wit' heem.'

'Please stop referring to me as though I was an inanimate object,' protested Smith.

'You see, heem's no good,' expostulated Pedro. 'Eef he gots dronk, *quién sabe?* He ees nots talk sense. Anyways, we only go from ver' short while. Nobody mees us.'

'All right, Pedro. Mak' sure he ees tied tight. Then we go.'

'*Si. Muchos gracias*.' Pedro tugged at Smith's bonds. 'Heem feexed tight. We go now.'

Smith watched the two Mexicans leave and, moments later, heard their horses gallop away. He was sure they had not locked the door. Either there was no lock, or they had forgotten it in their excitement. He strained at the ropes binding his wrists behind the chair, but they were firmly knotted. After a few moments of futile struggling he gave up and returned to contemplating his fate.

The three men who had brought him as far as the cabin had turned him over to the Mexicans and left immediately after exchanging a few words. The Mexicans had removed his blindfold and tied him in the chair. At first he had tried pumping his new captors for information, but apart from telling him that he would be there for only a day or so, he had learned nothing. They seemed much more interested in squabbling between themselves than in talking to him. Not that he understood much of what they said, anyway, even though their conversation consisted almost entirely of broken English.

Eventually he just sat back and kept quiet. They had untied him twice to feed him, but each time had replaced the ropes on his wrists. They had, however, neglected to bother with his feet. He had dozed in the chair, listening to the rain all night, and was by now sore and tired.

There had never been any hope of escape. The cabin appeared to consist of one room only, so sparsely furnished that Pedro had, after much arguing, slept on the only couch and Miguel on the floor. It seemed to him that both had tried to outdo each other in a snoring competition.

According to Miguel, he would be left alone for three or four hours, he reflected. Maybe longer if the Mexicans met up with some of their *amigos* and got drunk. Plenty of time to saw through his bonds and effect an escape.

He searched the scant furnishings of his prison with his eyes. The table, couch and pot-bellied stove seemed to offer no hope, and the floor was bare. Something niggled at his mind, something one of his captors had mentioned moments before leaving.

He went over their conversation as best he could remember it. After a few minutes he knew what it was. The bottle of *tequila*! If he could find the bottle, smash it and cut his bonds on the broken glass, he was free! Looking round the room again, his eyes alighted on a small cupboard to his left. Dragging the chair over to it, he examined the knob. It was too large to get his teeth round, and his hands would not reach. Desperately he tried to turn it by rubbing his head against it, then his shoulders. It would not budge. In frustration, he kicked at the cupboard, and in doing so toppled the chair backwards and he fell under the table. Standing up, he cracked his head on the corner of the table, groaned and sat down on the chair again. A trickle of blood ran down his nose into his mouth. He tasted the salt with his tongue.

When the pain had subsided, he collected his thoughts again. The table had a sharp edge, sharp enough to cut his scalp. Turning his back to the table, he raised his hands as far as they could go behind his back and commenced rubbing his bonds on the corner of the table.

It was a long, laborious task and several times he had to rest, his wrists sore and bleeding from the constant friction. After about an hour he felt a strand snap, and then another. Working furiously then, it took another half an hour for the remaining strands to wear through, and then he managed to struggle out of the ropes altogether. He sat gasping for another minute and then stood up, stretched his weary muscles, and strode over to the door. As he had suspected, it was not locked and thankfully he opened it and went outside.

★ ★ ★

Zeke sat studying the cabin from a hundred yards' distance. There were no horses, no sign of habitation. His fingers went to his pocket and felt the expensive necklace and brooch he had found at separate points along the trail. He knew they must belong to Smith, and that they had not been dropped accidentally. Smith would realise that someone would come looking for him and had the sense to leave pointers for them.

He dismounted, dropped the reins, and crept warily towards the cabin. Listening intently at the door, he heard nothing. There was no window, but quite a few chinks in the woodwork through which the, by now, strong sunlight entered the room. He peered through one of them and saw that the cabin was, indeed, empty of people. Entering, he saw at once what must have happened. The strands of rope still attached to the chair told him Smith had managed to escape; but where were his captors? Probably taken off after him. Zeke's mind boggled at the thought of the Easterner overpowering Westerners, even if they were only two crazy Mexicans, as Repeater had described them. He looked in the cupboard and found provisions for about a week, along with a bottle of *tequila* and an old oil lamp. So they would be back.

Zeke left the cabin, walked back to his horse, chose a suitable spot behind a clump of greasewood, sat down on a flat-topped boulder, and took out his corncob. No-one had passed him on the trail, so they had all obviously gone in the other direction. They would return that way, with or without their prisoner.

He lit his pipe and with the infinite patience of an Indian, settled down to wait.

★ ★ ★

The sun was already sinking towards the west when Pedro and Miguel sighted the entrance to Greasewood Canyon.

'W'at I tell you, *mi hermano?*' Pedro asked. 'We gots back no trouble. Nobody sees us, we have good time, no?'

Miguel did not answer, his eyes glassy, his thoughts far away.

'Oh, I theenk you more dronks that I am,' went on Pedro. 'You dronks weeth your Maria, I only dronks weeth *tequila* and *cerveza.*'

At the mention of his beloved Maria, Miguel seemed to come alive. 'Maria is *muy* pretty *señorita.* I theenk she lofe me.'

'*Si*, she lofe you. She lofe all *vaqueros*, I theenk.'

156

'You watch your tongue,' snarled Miguel. 'Eef you not dronks, I keel you.'

'*Lo siento. Si*, I am dronks. I am so dronks, I see theengs which you don' see.'

A while back, Pedro thought he had seen a figure move behind a bush, but when Miguel looked, he had seen nothing.

'You better be dronks. Eef the prisoner *escapa*, eet ees your fault. I tol' you to stay weeth heem, but no, you had to come. You check heem, tied tights, no?'

'*Si*,' muttered Pedro. 'He weel be there, Miguel.'

But he was not.

Miguel was first to dismount and enter the cabin. 'Caramba!' he shrieked, and Pedro stumbled drunkenly through the door after him. They stared stupefied at the empty chair.

'You fool,' moaned Miguel. 'He ees went.'

Pedro lurched over to the cupboard.

'Ah! The *tequila* ees still 'ere.' He took a long swig.

Miguel struck him viciously across the mouth with the back of his hand. Pedro reeled, clutching the bottle.

'W'at that for?' he gasped.

'You theenk more about that bottle than our hides,' Miguel told him. 'The *vaqueros* weel keel us. We mus' find heem *pronto*.'

''Ow we know where he go?' Pedro wanted to know.

'There ees *dos* ways from thees canyon. We weel go from Brent Crik or Peaceful. You go *uno* way, I go other. We find.'

'He don' know thees country,' objected Pedro. 'He go anywhere, mebbe lost.'

'We follow hees tracks, stupid. He weel not know 'ow to cover them. Come, before eet ees *oscuro*.'

Before his brother could reply, the door burst open and a giant figure filled the opening.

'*Madre de Dios!*' gasped Miguel.

Pedro gaped, unable to speak.

One stride and Zeke had the petrified Pedro's six-shooter. He levelled it at Miguel.

'Drop yore gunbelt, *pronto*,' he barked.

The Mexican complied at once.

'Now,' said Zeke, kicking the gunbelt in the corner, 'tell me what yuh've done with Mr. Smith.'

'*No entiendo*,' Miguel said sullenly.

Zeke stuffed Pedro's gun in his belt, stretched out his huge arms, and seized both of them by their shirts.

'If'n yuh don't tell me *muy pronto*, *amigos*, I'll cave both yore empty heads in.'

Pedro found his voice at last. 'We don' know where he ees, *señor*. We jus' gots back, an' he ees *arriba* an' went.'

'Who's payin' yuh to keep him here?'

'*Mucho malo hombre*.' This from Miguel, who had decided to give the answers in case his drunken brother gave too much away.

'I daresay,' said Zeke drily, 'but

what's his name?'

Miguel could not shrug his shoulders, due to being held an inch above the floor by Zeke's iron fist. '*Quién sabe?*'

'What does he look like, then?' Zeke asked grimly. 'An' if'n I don't git a straight answer this time — ' He left the threat unfinished.

'We don' know, *señor*. All we see ees *hombres* weeth *máscaras*.'

'Masks, eh? Well, if'n I find out yuh've been lyin' to me, yuh won't be safe in either *Estados Unidas de América* or *Méjico. Entiendo* that?'

Both brothers nodded vigorously, and Zeke dropped them. He picked up Miguel's pistol and stuffed it in his belt, alongside his brother's weapon.

'That gun, eet billong from me,' protested Miguel.

'Not any more, it don't,' Zeke informed him. 'Take off yore boots, both of yuh.'

'W'at for you want boots?' Pedro asked. 'They not feet you.'

'No, but yuh'll not be walkin' far

without 'em, I'll warrant.'

'Walkeeng? You take our *caballos*, too?'

'Yeah, for a while. Mebbe they'll come back, but if they've got any real hoss-sense they'll high-tail it right outa the county.'

Resignedly Miguel and Pedro took off their boots and gave them to Zeke.

'*Buenas tardes, señors*,' he said mockingly. 'An' don't fergit what I said. *Hasta luego*.' With that he was gone.

Miguel and Pedro looked at each other glumly. No boots, no horses, no prisoner. When the masked *vaqueros* returned, probably no Moreno brothers.

Zeke rode quickly north-west along the canyon, leading the Mexicans' horses. There was no need to look for tracks until he was out of the canyon: even so, he had spotted Smith's shoeprints, easily distinguished from the welter of hoofmarks along the trail. Discarding the pistols and the boots in the creek, he led the horses to the canyon entrance and released them.

They started grazing immediately, showing no inclination to hurry back to their Mexican owners. Zeke spurred his horse into a gallop in the wake of Frank Smith.

* * *

The employees of Smith's Pickles would have had great difficulty in recognising the proprietor of the firm had they been able to see him right now. Dirty, dishevelled, dusty, thirsty and hungry, he looked more like a hobo than a successful Boston businessman, and he was beginning to feel like one, too. He hobbled painfully along the rutted track by the creek, his eyes red and stinging from the dust which the sun had metamorphosised from the muddy bank of a short while ago, his throat was raw and his tongue felt swollen inside his mouth. His whole body ached and sweat ran in rivulets down his face and neck and dried almost immediately.

He was fantasising for the umpteenth

time on a huge flagon of cool beer, when he saw, indistinctly through the heat haze, a collection of buildings ahead that could only herald the start of something the Westerners would call civilisation. And after the agony of the last few hours Smith was prepared to welcome it as the very gates of Heaven.

With a silent, though heartfelt, prayer, he forced his tortured legs to a slightly faster pace and ran a parched tongue along his cracked lips.

Brent Creek was no larger than Peaceful, and certainly no prettier. The dingy-looking saloon-cum-dance-hall which overshadowed the other buildings on the main street went by the euphemism of the Palace. Skinny Bartles, the proprietor, looked up and eyed the apparition which had just entered.

'Gawd!' he exclaimed. 'Yuh look as if yuh'd jist walked across a desert, stranger.'

Frank Smith removed his dust-covered derby and mopped his brow with a grimy handkerchief. 'You could say that, friend, indeed you could. Can you oblige me with a drink of water?'

'Water?' queried the astonished Skinny, his jaw dropping. 'We ain't never had a request fer that. Will yuh settle fer a beer?'

'I'm afraid I haven't the wherewithal, even for a beer,' replied Smith.

'On the house,' Skinny proclaimed, sensing an interesting story was to come from this educated down-and-out. He set the beer on the bar and Smith gulped it down.

'Thank you,' he said, 'that was marvellous.'

'How come yuh didn't drink water from the crik, if'n yo're that thirsty?' Skinny wanted to know.

Smith shuddered. 'It was all muddy. In any case, I never thought of doing that,' he added lamely.

Skinny was burning with curiosity. 'What in hell's name were you doin' in these parts with no hoss?'

'It's a long story,' Smith said. 'I've got

to get back to Peaceful as soon as possible.'

'Stage don't go that way till Wednesday. What yuh gonna do till then?'

'I don't know. I don't suppose you can put me up? I've plenty of money, really, but I can't get hold of any just now, I'm afraid.'

'We-ell, if'n yuh ain't got collateral . . . Yuh know anybody in Brent Creek?'

'No. I came through here last Wednesday, on the stage, but we only made a short stop. I didn't speak to anyone.'

'The stage-driver, Luke Simms? You know him?'

'Yes, I remember Luke. A little, bow-legged — '

'Well then, if'n Luke can vouch fer yuh, it'll shore be all right fer yuh to stay.'

'Do you know where I can find him?' asked Smith.

'Shore. He ain't here, so he'll be in the saloon across the street. On'y two in town,' chuckled Skinny.

'Thanks, I'll go and get him.'

'Bring him over here. There's another free beer when yuh get back. I want to hear that long story,' called Skinny, as Smith left.

9

Alice rushed to meet Buck as he arrived at the PF ranch.

'Hello, Buck — or is it Zeke? I forget which — '

'I'm Buck, ma'am. Zeke is the one built like a house.'

'Oh, yes. And Frank — er, Mr. Smith? Do you know where he is? He was supposed to visit me yesterday, but he never showed up.'

Buck dismounted and tethered his horse to the hitching-rail. 'That's what I want to talk about, Mrs. Farrow. Mind if I come in?'

'Oh, please do. I'll put some coffee on.'

They went inside and Buck waited until the coffee was ready and Alice had seated herself opposite him.

'I'm afraid I ain't bearin' good news, ma'am,' he began. 'Yuh see, Frank never

made it here because, as he was ridin'
over, some fellers kidnapped him.'

'Oh, my God!' Alice blurted, her face
turning white. 'Have they hurt him?'

'We don't think so. Me an' Zeke
found the spot where it happened an'
Zeke went after 'em, him bein' the
better tracker, an' I came on here.' He
went on to tell of the note pinned on to
the sheriff's notice board and of
Johnny's subsequent surrender to the
sheriff.

'So they'll release Frank when they
know that Johnny is in jail?'

'I wouldn't count on it,' Buck replied
drily. 'Kidnappers ain't noted for
stickin' to promises.'

'Oh, dear. But what can they possibly
gain by holding on to him? Oh, of
course, he's got money, hasn't he? But
they won't hurt him, will they?'

'I shouldn't think so, ma'am,' Buck
reassured her. 'They've nothin' to gain
by that.'

'And Johnny didn't run away. I'm
glad about that. He must have found a

hide-out somewhere locally.'

'Yeah, he's been stayin' at the Bar L. But don't tell the sheriff, he's liable to take it the wrong way.'

'I might have known Margaret would put him up. They're kindly people, and Johnny's a nice boy.' She lapsed into silence for a while, her thoughts taking over.

'I'll be glad when the whole mess is settled,' she went on finally. 'Meanwhile, life has to go on, and I reckon it's coming up to lunch time. Will you stop and have some?'

'I'll be glad to, ma'am,' said Buck. 'Mind if I look around outside while you're preparin' it?'

'No, go ahead. There's not much to see, though, the ranch has just come to a standstill since Dan was shot.'

Buck wandered outside and nosed around the outbuildings. The bunkhouse, stables and corral all yielded nothing, and then something about fifty yards away caught his eye. He walked over to it and discovered it was a well.

Peering down, he saw it was deep and there was water in the bottom. Then his eyes narrowed as he noticed a patch of loose bricks about seven feet above the water line. Thoughtfully, he strolled back into the ranch house.

'I'm afraid there's quite a few repairs need to be done, but what with one thing and another I've not — ' began Alice as she appeared from the kitchen.

'Don't worry about that jist now,' Buck told her. 'This thing will all be straightened out pretty quick, I'm sure.'

'Did you see anything interesting?' Alice asked him.

'Yeah. Was yore husband a tall man, Mrs. Farrow?'

'Why, yes, he was.' Alice seemed surprised at the question. 'Quite a bit over six feet. But, why?'

'Jist somethin' that struck me, ma'am,' Buck answered vaguely. 'What do you know about that well out back?'

'Just that it's an ordinary well — where we get our water from. It's a good one, never dries up.'

'I'd like to take a look down there sometime, when my pardner's with me, if'n that's all right with you, ma'am.'

'Yes, of course. But I don't know what you'll find down there, apart from water,' replied Alice with a puzzled frown.

'Jist a hunch, thassall,' said Buck.

They ate lunch, during which Alice told Buck of Bram Ewell's latest visit and his proposition, which she had refused.

'Good for you, ma'am,' Buck enthused. 'That *hombre*'s up to no good, I'll be bound. I'd sooner trust a rattler.'

'I never did like him, Buck. He went away angry, saying that he'd get his hands on this ranch one way or another.'

'He threatened yuh?' Buck's hands clenched in anger.

'Well, not exactly. But it was a sort of veiled threat.'

'The swine! Me an' him's gonna have a showdown soon, that's fer shore!'

'Don't do anything rash, please,' Alice implored. 'He's got some pretty mean hands on his ranch.'

'I know, I've met some of 'em,' Buck agreed grimly. 'But don't worry about me, I'll be careful. We never see him in the Bald Eagle, have yuh any idea where he spends his evenin's?'

'Brent Creek, I think. Either the Palace or the Silver Spur. They're the saloons,' she explained.

Buck grinned. 'I can imagine,' he said. 'Well, thanks for the meal, ma'am. I guess I'll be ridin' now an' see what Zeke's been up to.'

'You don't think he's in trouble, do you?' Alice said anxiously.

'He's a few years outa diapers, but sometimes he forgets he don't carry a gun. He'll be all right,' Buck added as he saw the look on the widow's face.

'You will be careful, won't you? I just don't know what I'd do if anything happened to you, you seem so — so capable.'

Buck studied the widow critically. She

172

appeared agitated and he was reluctant to leave her in that state.

'Tell yuh what, ma'am,' he said at length. 'There's a section o' fence down, by the corral. Probably yesterday's storm caused it. I'll stay an' repair it fer yuh, if'n yuh like.'

★ ★ ★

Zeke rode into Brent Creek aware that Frank Smith must have arrived before him. Even an Easterner, after the trek across the rough terrain, would call first at a saloon to slake his thirst. There were two such establishments almost opposite each other on the main street — the Palace on the right, and a less imposing-looking edifice called the Silver Spur on the left. The big cowboy hitched his horse outside the latter.

Luke Simms spotted him the moment he shoved his huge frame through the batwing doors.

'Zeke!' the stage-driver called. 'What in tarnation are yuh doin' here?'

Zeke's eyes scanned the small crowd at the bar and picked out the speaker. 'I'm lookin' fer Frank Smith,' he said.

Luke looked puzzled. 'Yuh think the kidnappers've got him in Brent Creek?'

Zeke grinned. 'Nope. He ain't kidnapped no more, Luke. He escaped an' I follered him here.'

'What'll it be, stranger?' the bartender piped up.

Zeke ordered a beer and turned back to Luke.

'Well, he ain't in here,' said the stage-driver. 'Chances are he went in the Palace. We oughta mosey over there when yuh've finished yore drink.'

Zeke took a long draught. 'Yeah, I guess — ' He stopped short as the doors swung open.

'No need to,' he grinned. 'Here he is now.'

Smith sighed audibly with relief when he saw Zeke and Luke at the bar.

'Am I glad to see you two!' he exclaimed.

'Likewise,' said Zeke. 'Hell, that was

some walk yuh took.'

'Yes, I had no idea where I was heading at first — I just wanted to get away from those Mexicans.' Smith grinned. 'I bet they were surprised to find I was gone.'

'They were surprised all right,' Zeke affirmed. 'More so when I turned up an' discomforted 'em.'

'Why do you suppose they kidnapped me? Were they after a ransom?'

Zeke shook his head. 'No, that wasn't it, Mr. Smith. It was Johnny they were after. They pinned a note outside the sheriff's office, sayin' that unless Johnny surrendered hisself to the sheriff you could order yore pinebox.'

Smith paled. 'Buck told me he knew where Johnny was hiding out. Did he tell him about the note?'

'No need to. Word gits around pretty quick an' Johnny high-tailed it over to Sheriff Rawlins an' gave himself up.'

'Then he's in jail now? And safe?'

'He shore is. Lemme git yuh a beer, Mr. Smith. Yuh look as if yuh need it.'

Zeke and Smith swapped tales over another beer apiece while Luke listened carefully, storing away the details which he would embellish with gusto when the time came.

'If you can loan me a little of the money I've been paying you, Zeke, I can repay the gentleman in the other saloon for the beer I had there,' Smith said at length.

'Shore thing, but yuh ain't got to wait for the stage now. My hoss'll stand a little more weight, I guess.'

'That's great, I do want to get back and clean up and then see Alice — '

'Now, hold on. We ain't gonna let yuh go traipsin' round the country on yore own — yuh might attract a heap o' trouble again.'

'I suppose you're right,' admitted Smith. 'It is a little different from Boston out here.'

Luke placed his glass on the bar. 'C'mon then. I'm pretty shore Skinny owes me a drink. He'll be bustin' to hear the news.'

They heard the voice of Bram Ewell as they entered the Palace. He had his back to them and was addressing Skinny and another man at the bar.

'As soon as that murderin' rustler is strung up, Alice will see things differently. When we get hitched, we'll have the biggest spread in the county.' He poured himself another whiskey, a little unsteadily, and lit a cigar. He had not noticed the newcomers' arrival.

'Yessir, I reckon yuh can put all the trouble in these parts down to that Johnny Smith. Now he's behind bars — '

Frank Smith, his face white and eyes blazing, strode over to the rancher and confronted him. 'Johnny Smith never rustled any cattle or killed anybody, and you've got no right to accuse him.'

Ewell turned and viewed the still dishevelled Easterner with some surprise.

'An' jist who the hell are you?' he demanded.

'I'm Johnny's father.'

Ewell gasped and paled visibly. 'Yuh can't be. I — '

'You what, Mr. Ewell?'

The rancher then saw Zeke, glared at him, and without finishing his drink, stalked out of the saloon.

Skinny scratched his scrawny neck and pulled a wry face. 'Well, if'n this ain't got me beat all ends up,' he declared. 'You gents jist gotta fill me in on what the hell is happenin' around here.'

'If'n yuh'll jist set 'em up, Skinny, I'll tell yuh,' offered Luke.

'Shore thing, Luke. Two beers an' a rye comin' up. An' don't miss anythin' out.'

Luke launched into a colourful description of the events of the past few days, interspersed with some toning down comments by Zeke and Frank Smith. When he had finished, Skinny chuckled.

'I guess them greasers have shore landed themselves in a heap o' trouble. If'n they want to keep their hides in one piece I reckon they'd better hightail it back acrost the border *muy pronto*.'

'They gotta find their hosses fust,' said Zeke. 'An' then catch 'em. They're a mighty worried pair o' *hombres*.'

* * *

After taking his leave of Alice Farrow, Buck started back towards Peacful, but when he reached the spot where the ambush of Frank Smith had taken place, he decided to follow Zeke's trail while there was still plenty of daylight left. Zeke and his horse's combined weight had made deep tracks in the still moist ground and would be easy to trail.

The route took him to within a few hundred yards of the BE ranch, and as he approached he saw three riders leave the ranch and ride off in a north-westerly direction, exactly the course he was taking. Intrigued, he studied the ranch building, but saw no sign of life within.

Going more cautiously now and

trying to keep out of sight of the riders, he followed. The distance was too great to recognise any of them, but he could see that none of them suspected he was behind them, as they rode openly at a fast pace and looking ahead all the time. He could still make out Zeke's horse's tracks, even though the trail here was much more heavily used, and Buck suspected it was the main one from the BE ranch to Brent Creek.

A few miles farther on the three riders in front veered westward at the mouth of a canyon, but Buck noticed that Zeke's tracks led straight into the canyon, along with a few others. After a moment's hesitation, he decided to enter the canyon and follow his sidekick. That was, he told himself, his primary intention after all. He was still curious about the three horsemen, but decided they were in too much of a hurry to pick their way along the canyon floor, and would probably rejoin the trail at the other end.

When he was well into the canyon he

came across a cabin, which proved to be empty. There was a welter of tracks around this area, many of them fairly fresh. And then he spotted shoeprints, leading north-west. They were definitely not those made by cowboy boots, but more like shoes worn by people in the cities. Could they belong to Frank Smith? If so, what was he doing walking alone in that direction? Surely if Zeke had rescued him from this cabin they would have ridden double.

Baffled, he continued down the canyon, both Zeke's tracks and the tracks of the men on foot quite distinguishable from the others.

He had just left the canyon behind and was following the course of the muddy creek when he saw two figures wading in the murky waters. Riding close, he saw they were both Mexicans and looking very sorry for themselves.

Reining his horse, he called to them. '*Buenos tardes, hombres*. Havin' a nice paddle?'

One of the Mexicans was carrying a

sodden boot. 'We're looking for *botas*, *señor*. We nots paddle.'

'How come yuh lost yore boots in the creek?' Buck wanted to know.

'We were attacked, *señor*,' replied the more talkative Mexican. 'By *muy beeg hombre*. He take our *caballos*, too. You nots see them, no?' he added hopefully.

That sounded like they had met up with Zeke, thought Buck.

'No, I ain't seen yore hosses. Why did this big feller attack yuh? Jist to pinch yore boots an' chuck 'em in the creek?'

'Si, that's it, *señor*. Heem's *mucho malo hombre*. He take our pistols as well.'

'I suspect you two was up to no good an' he taught yuh a lesson,' said Buck. 'Sorry I can't stop to chat, fellas. Good huntin'.' He spurred his horse and left the Mexicans gesticulating and shouting after him.

★ ★ ★

182

It was growing dark when Ewell and a pair of unprepossessing punchers, Jim Dawson and Al Schwarz, hitched outside the Palace.

'Now don't fergit what I tol' yuh,' the rancher said. 'Bull's mistake was that he didn't leave space between hisself an' that big ape. Jim, you watch the stage-driver, he could be armed. Al, you take care of Henderson. When he makes his move, draw an' fire — yuh thought he had a gun, remember? I'll see to the Easterner.'

Ewell had figured the least danger would come from Smith. If bullets flew, or a fight developed, he would be out of the way. After that he would settle with those greasers and then there was just the gunfighter Lawrence to deal with; the most dangerous of the lot, thought Ewell. There must be no slip-ups next time. A slug from a marksman after Lawrence had been lured into a dark alley.

These thoughts flashed through the rancher's mind as he pushed open the batwings of the saloon. There were a few more customers slaking their thirsts now that sundown had arrived. Zeke, Smith and Luke were still there, propping the bar up and talking to Skinny.

Ewell ordered a bottle of rye and three glasses, poured drinks for Dawson and Schwarz, picked up the bottle and a glass and walked to the far end of the long bar. As he poured his own drink, he turned and looked insolently at the trio a few yards away. Then, downing his whiskey, he called to Skinny, 'Hey, barkeep, ain't there some kinda law that says yuh oughtn't to serve scum like that?'

Immediately a hush fell upon the customers as they looked at Zeke and then back to the newcomers. One or two backed away out of the line of fire. Zeke's huge hands clenched and unclenched in readiness and Luke eased his Colt in its holster.

Ewell addressed the proprietor again. 'I'm waitin' fer an answer, yuh scrawny galoot.'

Skinny gulped, but replied as dignified as he could.

'Anyone gets a drink here, providin' he has the money to pay for it,' he said.

'That lot don't look as if they've got two bits between them,' sneered Ewell. 'If they've got money, they musta robbed a bank.'

Frank Smith spoke up. 'Now look here — ' he began.

'No, you look here.' Ewell looked up and addressed the rest of the customers. 'Those two belong to a murderous gang who've been terrorisin' Peaceful, an' I wouldn't be surprised if'n the stage-driver ain't in on it, too. Why, the funny-dressed one is the old man of a feller in jail for murder over in Peaceful. Ain't that so, yuh sonofabitch?'

The tension in the air was a tangible thing. The tableau held, no-one moving, no-one breathing. At one end of the bar Ewell stood waiting, flanked by Dawson and Schwarz, their hands hovering over their holstered guns. At the other end the white-faced Smith stood seething and helpless, alongside the giant, who was like a coiled spring, and the little stage-driver whose eyes flickered round the room, watching for who would break first. Death threatened several people, with the odds stacked heavily against Smith and his companions.

Smith broke first, taking a quick step towards Ewell. Zeke moved to stop him, and Schwarz's hand flew to his gun.

The roar of a Colt shattered the silence and Schwarz screamed, his hand smashed to a bloody pulp. Gunsmoke drifted from the doorway and all eyes turned to see Buck holstering his gun.

'Seems like I arrived jist in time,' he said. 'This feller was drawin' on an unarmed man. That's murder in my book.'

He strolled over to the bar, ignoring the cursing Schwarz.

'Yuh couldn'ta timed it better, Buck,' Luke enthused. 'Another second an' there'd a' been all hell to pay. What'll yuh have to drink?'

Buck grinned. 'This I can't refuse. I'll

have a whiskey.'

'Look what yuh done to my hand,' howled Schwarz, extending his arm, which ended in a mass of blood. 'It's useless.'

Buck's green eyes regarded him steadily. 'Yeah, yuh won't be shootin' any unarmed men with it now, will yuh?' he said coldly. 'Think yoreself lucky I hadn't a mind to perforate yore shirt.'

Ewell kept quiet, having a healthy respect for Buck's gun. But Dawson had never met Buck before and had not seen him draw. All he knew was that the lean cowpuncher had fired when no-one was looking and had all the time in the world to take aim at his partner's hand.

'Yuh hadn't oughta butted in like that, feller,' Dawson rasped. 'It woulda been a fair fight.'

Buck took a drink of his whiskey, placed the glass down carefully, and turned to face Dawson.

'If'n you draw on me now, *hombre*,' he said, his voice full of menace, '*that'll* be a fair fight.'

There was a scrabbling of chairs and boots as the area was cleared for a second time. Dawson was not without courage and had faced dangers before, but there was something about this calculating stranger that unnerved him. The challenge had been made, but the BE cowboy hesitated. The newcomer could shoot, Al Schwarz was witness to that, but how fast was he on the draw? There was only one way to find out.

Before he could move, the doors burst open again and Bull Bartram's beefy figure entered. His hands dropped to his twin Dragoon .44s as he took in the situation.

'Havin' trouble, Boss?' he called to Ewell. 'Is the gunfighter threatenin' yuh?'

Buck was now menaced from both sides and the situation was fraught with danger. Bartram must have seen him pass the ranch and followed him here, as he had followed Ewell and his boys. He could not shoot Dawson and

Bartram with his single Peacemaker before one of them got him. He cursed his lack of foresight in placing himself between the door and Ewell. If he fired and dived, Smith, Zeke or Luke could easily stop a bullet.

Nobody paid any attention to Skinny Bartles as the bartender bent down behind the bar, but they did when he straightened up and they found themselves looking down the twin barrels of a ten-gauge shotgun.

'There'll be no more drawn guns in this saloon,' Skinny said, his voice surprisingly steady. He swung the shotgun towards Ewell and his cronies. 'Yuh may be a good customer, Mr. Ewell, but yuh ain't the only one. Seein' as how you started this ruckus I'm orderin' yuh to leave right now, an' take yore hirelings with yuh.'

For a moment nobody moved and then, with a sigh, Ewell started for the door. 'C'mon, boys, let's get that hand attended to. Seems like we ain't welcome in here any more.'

Bartram appeared about to protest, but Ewell shoved him through the doors and into the street. A cowpoke leaned his head over the batwings and watched them unhitch their horses, mount and ride away into the night.

''S all right, they've gone,' he announced, and there was an audible expellation of air as the customers relaxed.

'Good thing yuh kept that scattergun under the bar,' Buck said to Skinny. 'But would yuh have used it indoors? Yuh would have blown Ewell's head off, shore, but a whole passel o' customers woulda caught it, most of which wouldn't look very pretty afterwards.'

Skinny grinned and wiped the sweat from his brow with the barcloth. 'That's a dangfool question, Mister. It ain't even loaded!'

10

Buck, Zeke and Frank Smith spent the night at the Palace and rode back to Peaceful the next morning, Smith riding double on Buck's Appaloosa. During the journey Smith expressed his desire to visit the jail and see his son, so as soon as they reached the town they hitched their horses outside the sheriff's office. Buck knocked on the door and waited.

The door remained closed, but from inside came the sound of muffled curses. After a couple of minutes, Buck opened the door and went in. The office was empty, but behind the bars of the jailhouse door, Moose Roberts stood, his face purple with anger and his expletives no less colourful.

'Lemme outa here,' he yelled, shaking the bars, 'I wanna git after that misbegotten cowpuncher. When I ketch up with him, I'll rearrange his face for him. I'll — '

Buck found the keys on the desk and unlocked the door. 'Now, hold on a minute, Depitty. Jist tell us what happened.' He could not refrain from grinning as he looked at the egg-sized lump poking through the deputy's sparse lank hair.

Ignoring him, Moose strode across the office and jerked the desk drawer open.

'Hmm,' he muttered. 'At least he left my gun.' He took out the old Army .44 and stuffed it into his belt. 'Took his own though, damn him.'

Zeke and Smith crowded in. 'What the hell's happened, Moose?' asked Zeke, surveying the room. 'You been havin' a party?'

'My haid feels like I had a real humdinger of a party, but my memory shore tells me a different tale.'

'Tell us, then,' Zeke invited, sitting gingerly on one of the office chairs.

Moose sat down behind the desk and

gently felt the lump on his head. 'Damn' cowpuncher,' he growled. 'When I ketch up with him I'll larn him to have more respect fer the law.'

Buck made a quirly, lit it and drew heavily. 'Quit moanin',' he ordered, 'an' git on with it.'

'Well,' Moose began somewhat ruefully, 'it was partly my fault, I suppose. Musta been after midnight, I was havin' a doze in the chair here, when I was woke up by an awful hollerin' from the cells. I was still half asleep, so I ambles over to ask him what all the ruckus was about when he grabs me an' lifts my gun. Then he orders me to get the keys an' unlock the door, which I do 'cause I ain't got no choice, seein' as he has my own gun pointin' straight at my middle. After that, I don't remember any more till I woke up in the cell feelin' like I been kicked in the haid by a mule, an' that jasper gone. Gawd, is he gonna suffer when I ketch him.'

'So Johnny's free again,' Frank Smith commented, stating the obvious. 'I'll lay odds he's gone looking for me. If only we had ridden back last night we might have saved you that headache, Mr. Roberts.'

'Yeah, yuh should'a done that, Mr. Smith,' agreed Moose, then suddenly realised to whom he had addressed the remark.

'Say, yo're free again, ain'tcha? What in tarnation happened to yuh?'

Smith and Zeke filled in the details between them, and when they had finished Moose pulled a wry face.

'So we still don't know who kidnapped yuh. Any chance of findin' those greasers, Zeke?'

'If'n they ain't over the border by sundown tonight, I reckon there's a pretty even chance yuh might find their bones in a washout someplace around. That's if the coyotes an' buzzards leave anythin' recognisable.'

Moose turned back to Smith. 'If'n yuh want me to lock yuh in the cells, Mr. Smith — for safety's sake, that is — I'd be pleased to oblige.'

'If'n yuh look after him like yuh did his son, I'll reckon he'll be a lot safer in the hotel,' said Buck.

Moose grinned for the first time. 'Yeah, I guess yo're right at that. But stay there, won't yuh, Mr. Smith, an' don't go gallivantin' about them hills on yore own till we've nailed those kidnappers. Next time they could be a darned sight rougher with yuh.'

'He's right, Mr. Smith,' Zeke put in. 'You don't know this country like we do, or the *hombres* that crawl out from under rocks when yuh ain't lookin'.'

Smith gave a wry smile. 'I do seem to have gotten myself in the thick of it, don't I? All right, Zeke, I'll keep out of the way until it's all over. I've had quite enough excitement for one week. As a matter of fact, there's been more happened to me since I arrived in Peaceful than has happened in the rest of my life up to now. But don't forget I haven't seen Johnny yet, and I'm not giving Alice up in a hurry, either.'

Buck and Zeke exchanged glances

and the giant changed the subject. 'I'm hungry enough to eat a hoss an' its rider,' he said. 'C'mon, fellers, let's go an' eat.'

★ ★ ★

After they had eaten a hearty pile of pancakes at a little Mexican eating-house and Frank Smith had been ensconced in the hotel with a further reminder not to leave town, Buck and Zeke headed out to the PF ranch.

'Are we jist checkin' that the widder's keepin' out of trouble, or is there some other reason?' Zeke asked Buck when they were well on the way.

'You got it, Zeke — there's some other reason.'

Zeke waited a moment, riding along in silence.

'Well,' he said at last, 'are yuh gonna tell me what it is — or is it so dad-blasted secret no-one's allowed to know?'

Buck looked at his partner through

narrowed lids and then gave a chuckle. 'It's jist a hunch, is all,' he admitted, 'an' I don't wanna commit myself by tellin' yuh about it.'

'Meanin' yo're gonna look an awful fool if'n yore hunch don't turn out, right?'

'Right.'

Alice was pleased, if a little surprised, to see them.

'I didn't expect you boys back so quickly,' she told them. 'Have you any news about Frank?' She appeared to have got over her embarrassment at using the Easterner's first name.

'Yes, ma'am, we shore have,' Zeke informed her. 'He's safe and well back in the hotel at present. We jist left him.'

'Oh, I'm so glad.' Her eyes sparkled with pleasure. 'Did you have much trouble rescuing him from the kid-nappers?'

Buck gave a short laugh. 'No trouble at all, ma'am. By the time Zeke caught up with him, he'd already escaped.'

Alice invited them in to tell her all

197

about it over lunch, an invitation that neither of them was reluctant to disdain.

When they had eaten their fill, Zeke methodically filled his pipe with Durham and Buck rolled a quirly. They lit up, Buck keeping his eyes fixed on Zeke and Alice.

'Now fer the real reason I dragged Zeke out here,' he said, drawing deeply.

'Yuh mean it wasn't for the grub?' Zeke's eyebrows took an exaggerated leap upwards.

Buck addressed Alice and ignored his partner completely. 'When I was here yestiddy, yuh said it would be all right if'n me an' Zeke took a look down that well out back.'

'Why, yes, of course, Buck. But I still don't see what you hope to find.'

'Even if we find nothin' down there, it's given me an idea to bring the troublemakers out into the open.' He chuckled to himself, and Zeke looked at him quizzically. 'C'mon, Zeke, you've got some work to do. Put that

198

pipe out an' foller me.'

'Aw, Buck, I only jist got it goin',' Zeke protested. 'In any case there ain't many jobs I can't do while I'm smokin' it.'

'Like climbin' down wells?'

Zeke pulled a wry face. 'Can't say I've tried that one. But I'll give it a shot.'

They walked out to the well and Buck pointed down to the patch of loose bricks above the water.

'Think yuh can get down an' take a look at those bricks — the ones that look kinda disturbed? Yuh can easily lodge yore shoulders an' feet on either side an' hold on to the rope as well. I'll hold it firm up this end. It's a bit on the wide side fer me, I might slip,' he explained in answer to Zeke's inquiring look.

Zeke sighed, and tapped his corncob on the wall of the well.

'I wish I knew what I'm supposed to be lookin' fer, but you shore as hell ain't gonna tell me, so I'd better go find out.'

He swung his legs over the wall, sat

on the rim and tugged at the rope above the bucket. 'Seems strong enough.'

Sliding his legs across to the far wall, he launched himself over the edge and braced his shoulders on the wall opposite.

'Right, Buck. Now, you lower the bucket ahead o' me, I don't want it crashin' down on top of my head when I'm half-way down.'

Buck grinned and ground his cigarette into the dust.

'Shore thing, pardner. I'd hate to give yuh a extry bath, considerin' yuh only had one a week ago.'

Buck manoeuvred the bucket past Zeke and the big puncher followed it down easily until he came to the patch of loose bricks.

'Pull the bucket alongside me,' Zeke called as he steadied himself, 'an then I can drop the bricks in it.'

When the bucket was level with his body, he gripped the rope with his left hand and pulled the first brick with his right. It came out easily. He loosened two others, dropped them into the bucket and put his hand in the resultant hole. His fingers scrabbled around for a moment, then touched something soft. Taking a firm grip, he pulled out a canvas bag, packed tight with what felt like paper.

'Hey, is this what we're lookin' for?'

'Could be,' came the reply. 'Drop it in the bucket an' we'll take a look.'

Zeke complied and Buck immediately hauled up the rope.

'What about me, I'm stuck down here?' shouted Zeke.

'Aw, you can climb up easy enough, I'll fix the bucket so's it don't drop on yuh.'

'Thanks a lot,' muttered Zeke and began levering himself up the well.

When he reached the top, Buck was waiting with a broad grin on his face.

'What you lookin' so smug about?' panted Zeke, as he hauled himself over the wall.

'I was right about the well,' said Buck. 'Take a look in here.'

Zeke sat on the edge of the well and dusted himself down with his sombrero. 'Lemme get my breath back. Now, what have I jist risked life an' limb for?'

Buck held up a packet tightly bound with rubber bands. 'Bills, all large denomination. Quite a few packets.'

Zeke whistled. 'How much do yuh reckon is there?'

'At a guess, twenty-three thousand dollars. This is the missing currency. Pete Farrow hid it here before he got shot. Mrs. Farrow said he didn't trust banks much.'

They went back to the ranch house.

'We found yore husband's money, Mrs. Farrow,' said Buck, tossing the canvas bag on to the table. 'It was down in the well all the time.'

Alice's eyes opened wide in amazement. 'Oh, thank you, boys. It's there, in that bag? How much do you think there is?'

'Better count it an' see, ma'am,' said Zeke. 'Shore is a hefty package.'

Alice fumbled with the drawstring

and then said, 'Will you do it for me? I seem to be shaking too much.'

Buck grinned and tipped the wads from the bag on to the table. Then he set to counting. After a few minutes he looked up.

'It's all there, ma'am. Twenty-three thousand.'

'Good heavens! That means I can save the ranch. I can — '

'Hold on there, ma'am. Don't yuh do anythin' hasty jist yet. I think I know how we can bring matters to a head. With yore permission, I'd like to use this money to bait a trap.'

'How do you mean, Buck?' asked Alice.

'Yeah,' said Zeke. 'What yuh got in mind, pard?'

'If'n yuh wanna catch somethin' — bear or fish, or whatever, yuh gotta use a suitable bait. Ain't that right?'

'Huh, I guess so,' Zeke agreed.

'Well, a big sum of money is the most suitable bait fer a gang of human thieves, or rustlers.'

'I can see that,' said Alice. 'But what's your plan?'

'There's no need to risk the money — that can be hidden safely again, only this time you'll know where it is, Mrs. Farrow. I propose we let the word spread that we've found the money and that we intend takin' it to the bank in Peaceful. The hardcases will stage a hold-up on the trail, but we'll have a little surprise waitin' fer 'em.'

'Isn't that dangerous? I mean, somebody could get killed,' Alice put in anxiously.

'That's a chance we gotta take. I notice you've got a flat-bottomed wagon out back, ma'am. If I drive, an' Zeke hides under a tarp in the well — '

'But Zeke doesn't carry a gun.'

'Have yuh got a shotgun he can borrow? Even Zeke can't miss with that, so long as he realises which end to point.'

'Yes, Pete's old twelve-bore's in an outhouse somewhere.'

'Good. I think mebbe we should enlist the help of the law, too. D'yuh reckon Moose Roberts could get in the wagon alongside Zeke?'

Alice smiled. 'I think there'll be room for both of them. It's a pretty large rig.'

'How do we let the bushwhackers know when we'll be headin' for town?' Zeke wanted to know. 'We can't go round tellin' everybody, it'd look mighty suspicious.'

'Sure, that's right, Zeke,' Buck answered. 'All we gotta do is jist let it slip out to one person — in friendly conversation. Now, who's the gabbiest gent we know in town?'

'Well, we've only been here a week an' we ain't met everybody, but I'm bettin' Luke Simms takes first prize.'

'You got it first time, big feller,' Buck grinned. 'Lemme see, today's Tuesday, ain't it? That means the stage will be due in tomorrow with a thirsty Luke ready to lap up any little gems o' gossip. If'n we take a ride into town then, we can go straight to work on the stage-driver.'

Zeke frowned. 'But Luke'll spread the news like wildfire. It'll be all over the territory by sundown. What if some enterprisin' owlhoots decide not to wait for us an' come lookin' for the cash at the ranch?'

'We'll be back here by then to guard Mrs. Farrow and the money — that is, if that's all right with you, ma'am?'

'You mean stay the night here? Oh, yes, I'll feel a lot safer with you boys here. Why don't you stay tonight as well? I feel a little nervous with all that money in the house.'

'Gee, thanks, Mrs. Farrow. But we'd better make ourselves useful an' earn our keep. I think we should ride over to the eastern range an' do a check on yore stock. We ain't covered that territory yet.'

'The grassland's not so rich over that way, Buck,' Alice told him. 'There's more hills and rocks, sage and grease-wood. In fact, it peters out after a few miles into real badlands. But at one time we had quite a herd grazing over there. I don't think you'll find much nowadays, though.'

'Nevertheless, we'll take a look. C'mon, Zeke, let's saddle up.'

11

The two cowboys reported back to the ranch before supper, telling Alice that she had a lot of stock, but the trouble was that most of it bore the BE brand.

'An' they're all mavericks,' Buck informed her. 'If'n they're all over yore range, ma'am, like they seem to be, yuh've got the makin's of a decent herd.'

'You keep giving me new hope,' Alice said, her eyes shining. 'Finding all that money for me, and telling me that I've not lost all my cattle. I really thought at one time I would have to sell up and leave, but I'm determined that Bram Ewell won't get his hands on the ranch. Yes, I'd certainly like to get started again, if at all possible. If the rustlers are caught and dealt with properly, and I can get a few hands together again — well we'll have to see.'

Buck and Zeke slept in the bunk-house after supper and were awake early next day, doing all the chores and cooking breakfast before Alice was up.

'Well, boys, this is a nice surprise,' she greeted as she sat down to bacon and eggs served by Zeke.

'No more 'n yuh deserve, ma'am,' said Zeke, 'seein' as how yuh looked after us. We got to make a start soon to attend to the business in town.'

Alice smiled. 'I'm sure you'll do a good job with the stage-driver,' she said.

★   ★   ★

As they rode towards Peaceful, Buck kept his eyes open for a possible spot for an ambush. The open rangeland afforded little cover; a few clumps of prickly pear, a little pine scrub and brush, but nothing near enough to the trail to hide a bunch of dry gulchers. There would be the cottonwoods, of course, at the bottom of the hill, but that was too near the town to risk shots.

When they were about three miles from town, Buck allowed himself a grim smile. This would be the spot, he'd wager. They were riding through a grassy swale, flanked on the right by a long, timbered ridge. Zeke came to the same conclusion at the same time.

'See them trees up on that ridge, Buck?' he said. 'Guess that's where they'll make their move. Any nearer town an' it'll be too dangerous fer 'em.'

'Yeah, but I think mebbe it's a little too far for accurate shootin', 'less they've got some extry special marksmen among 'em. They'll have to show 'emselves an' give us warnin'.'

'I wish Hank hadn't gone away,' Zeke reflected. 'We're a bit thin on the ground in the law department.'

'He should be back tomorrow, mebbe even today. He'll shore enough be back to arrange our funerals, if'n things go wrong.'

Zeke grinned wryly. 'Thanks for cheerin' me up, pardner.'

Twenty minutes later they hitched

their horses outside the sheriff's office. Moose Roberts let them in.

'Howdy, Depitty,' greeted Buck. 'How's the haid?'

Moose felt the offending lump gingerly and winced. 'It's stopped throbbin', I jist gotta remember not to touch it. Doc says it'll be all right in a day or two, but I can't get my hat on yet. You boys got any news?'

They outlined their plan to the deputy, who eventually agreed to participate after getting Zeke to promise not to go near Moose's head with any part of his anatomy while they were under the tarpaulin.

'I'll sneak out before sunup, headin' fer the Bar L, in case anyone spots me, then circle round back o' the cotton-woods. I'll be up at the Widder's in time fer breakfast. Hell, I shore wish Hank was here, he'd know what to do. He did say I was to trust you boys, though.'

'That's right, Moose. Hank will shore approve what yo're doin',' Buck assured him.

Moose's long, morose features showed no sign whether he thought the sheriff would approve or not.

* * *

The two punchers ate in the hotel dining-room and brought Frank Smith up to date on the situation. He was delighted that they had discovered the whereabouts of Alice's money, but held reservations about the sagacity of their plan to trap the wrongdoers.

'It seems a risky business to me, boys,' he said. 'You could get yourselves killed, and where would that leave Alice, or me and Johnny for that matter?'

'Don't yuh fret, Mr. Smith,' Zeke told him. 'We'll be all right.'

To take the Boston man's mind away from the dire possibilities of tomorrow, Buck suggested they rope Pete McCall, the receptionist, in for a game of penny-ante poker. Pete consented and they spent the afternoon playing cards, smoking and telling each other tall stories.

When the thunderous cacophony in the street outside announced the arrival of Luke and the Concord, Buck and Zeke exchanged glances and shoved the cards to the centre of the table.

'Thanks for the game, gents,' said Buck. 'I think we'll mosey over to the saloon now for a little refreshment.'

They met Luke as he was bow-legging it to the Bald Eagle. Buck drew the little stage-driver aside and whispered conspiratorially, 'We want yuh to do somethin' fer us, Luke. We can trust yuh, can't we?'

'Shore, gents, anythin' I can do to help. Is it to help catch the hardcases?'

'That's right, Luke. Now, me an' my buddy here are goin' in the saloon to do a little imbibin', same as you are. We got a heavy day ahead tomorrow. What we want yuh to do is keep an eye, or rather an ear, open for any slips we might make.'

'How's that, Buck? I don't foller yuh.'

'Well,' Buck looked around at the

empty street in an exaggerated fashion. 'If we so much as breathe a word about any large sums of money, we want you to shut us up — stamp on my foot, knock Zeke's beer over, anythin' to remind us to clam up. *Sabe?*'

'Yeah, I got it. But, why? What money are yuh talkin' about?'

Again Buck performed his hyperbolic act. 'We didn't want to tell anyone, but I guess we can trust you, can't we, Zeke?'

'If'n we can't trust Luke, we can't trust anybody,' Zeke stated, blank-faced.

'Have you boys come into money?' Luke tried an inspired guess.

'Shhh! No, not us. But we found the widder's money — the cash from her husband's last round-up. Twenty-three thousand dollars.'

'Wow! Twenty-three th — '

'Shhh! We ain't talkin' about it, remember.'

'Sorry, boys. I'll keep quiet. Not a word!'

'That the idea. I'm bringin' it to the

bank tomorrow mornin'. I'll be usin' a buckboard, or some such, to make it look like I'm fetchin' supplies for the widder. Zeke'll stay an' keep guard on the ranch.'

'Ain't it risky, travellin' to town with all that currency?'

'Why should it be? Nobody'll know I've got it, will they?'

'No. 'Course not. C'mon, let's git to drinkin'. My mouth feels like the Arizony desert itself.'

The Bald Eagle was fairly well patronised by that time of day and the Bar L crowd was already ensconced at the poker table. Luke allowed Buck to buy his first drink in payment for the favour the stage-driver was performing. They waited until Luke was well into his third drink (and third tall story), and then Buck and Zeke made their excuses and left, feeling sure that before the evening was over Luke would let slip about the trip to the bank tomorrow, probably unintentionally, and some big-eared bystander would latch on to it and word would get around the town like a prairie fire.

★ ★ ★

Buck took the first watch, basing himself in the kitchen and roaming round the ranch at intervals to keep himself awake and to check on all directions for a sneak attack. After he considered Zeke had had sufficient sleep, he crept into the bunkhouse and shook the slumbering giant awake.

'Yore turn to keep guard now, ol' buddy,' he said when he finally had Zeke fully cognizant.

'Huh? Yuh mean it's mornin' already?' was Zeke's opening remark. 'I'm disbelievin' yuh. It ain't even threatenin' daylight.'

'We agreed to share the guard duties, remember?' Buck sighed patiently. 'Yuh kin wake me when it's sunup.'

Zeke remembered where they were and grinned sheepishly.

'Sorry, Buck, I guess I was dreamin'.

216

Did yuh hear anythin'?'

'Only an owl, a coyote, an' yore snorin'.'

'Right. I'll let yuh sleep till Moose arrives an' breakfast is ready. That is, unless we have any uninvited visitors.'

★　★　★

Johnny Smith's feeling of exhilaration at being free was tempered by one of frustration in not knowing what was happening in the outside world. He had decided he could not spend another night in the cell while his father was out there somewhere in mortal danger. He deeply regretted having to knock out the deputy with his gun barrel, and realised that now he really had broken the law. After being cooped up on the Bar L ranch, then in jail, he had been almost crazy for the wide open spaces. Two days and nights roaming the hills and sleeping under the stars had relieved the pent-up feeling, but had not brought him any nearer to finding his father.

He had, however, come to a decision. Bram Ewell was mixed up in this business he was sure. Whether he was the sole instigator or not, Johnny did not know, but he had had a long time to ponder on the BE outfit, and had convinced himself that some of the answers lay at the Ewell ranch. He was headed there now, with no fixed plan, just determination to confront someone there — whoever he came across.

When he arrived at the peripheral fence of the ranch house Johnny found the only person in the outfit whom he would not accuse of anything: Repeater Riley. He liked him, and had always felt sorry that he had to find employment with such a mean bunch.

Repeater saw him as he rode up. 'Why hello, Mr. Smith, Johnny. Ain't see'd yuh fer quite a spell. Yuh been hidin' yoreself?' He laughed at his feeble, but unintentionally accurate joke. 'Quite a spell,' he added in his usual fashion.

'Yeah, that's right, Repeater. Is Mr. Ewell in the house, or Bull?'

'Nope, they've all took off, first thing this mornin'. First thing. Dunno where they went, though.'

'What, the whole danged outfit?'

Repeater screwed his face up, remembering. 'No, not all of 'em. The cook, he's still there. Oh, an' Al Schwarz — he cain't do nothin' 'cos of his busted hand. Yeah, that's it, busted hand.'

'That sonofabitch,' Johnny's lip curled. 'How'd he git it?'

'Got into a gunfight at Brent Crik a few nights ago. Gunfight.'

'Serve him right,' said Johnny unsympathetically. He had never liked the BE puncher.

'Watcha gonna do?' Repeater asked. 'Wait till they come back?'

'Yeah, I'll wait. But first I'll take care of Schwarz and the cook,' Johnny added grimly.

★   ★   ★

There were no visitors, welcome or otherwise, at the PF ranch until Moose

219

Roberts arrived about an hour after sunrise. The deputy was sure no-one had seen him leaving town, but he had headed out in the other direction for a mile or two just in case, before circling round to the north, then east.

There was an air of tension as they ate breakfast, each of them knowing that before the day was out one or all of them could have been injured or killed. Assuming the intending robbers fell for Luke's tale, the trio in the wagon would probably be outnumbered, perhaps heavily. They were relying purely on the element of surprise.

While the men had an after-breakfast smoke, Alice fetched her husband's shotgun and Buck checked that it was loaded in both barrels and that the firing mechanism and triggers worked properly. Moose had brought his Sharps' carbine and Buck had the Winchester.

They hitched the wagon to a pair of lively bay mares and Zeke and Moose climbed gingerly in the well, the deputy constantly reminding Zeke about his sore head and the giant continuously reassuring him he wouldn't move a muscle. Buck covered them with a tarpaulin, then took the reins with his rifle across his knees.

Alice came out to wish them luck and, feeling excessively conspicuous atop the high wagon, Buck set the horses in motion. The sun had climbed to a respectable height as the wagon reached the plateau above the ranch, and a skylark was in full song way up in the sky. The rangeland looked as peaceful as it ever had, but Buck was far too tense to notice any of these things. His preoccupation was with the death that could be lurking somewhere on that tranquil scene.

It would be no more than nine or ten miles to Peaceful along a mainly straightforward trail, but that morning it seemed more like ninety to Buck. He wondered briefly what it must seem like to the two sweating it out in the well of the wagon, covered by the tarp and unable to see a thing. At least he had his eyes, as well as his ears and every nerve alert for danger. He would be the first to know of an impending attack; well, he hoped he would. The thought of a bullet in the back, with no warning, brought a cold sweat to his brow, despite the heat of the sun.

Reaching the spot they had selected as the ambushers' best bet without incident, Buck murmured in a low voice, 'Git ready now, gents. I reckon this could be it.'

He kept his eyes on the treeline to his right, and when they were half-way along he saw a horseman break cover, followed by another, then another. They had let him pass by and were now galloping in from the rear, hoping he would not see them until he could hear the drumming of hoofbeats.

'Here they come,' he yelled as the leading rider also yelled, commanding Buck to stop. There were six horsemen he noted with dismay; would that be too many to cope with?

So as to leave him in no doubt as to their intentions, one of the riders, all of whom wore bandannas over their faces, fired a shot at him which missed by yards. As he snatched up his Winchester, Zeke and Moose threw back the tarpaulin, blinked in the bright sunlight, and desperately hoisted their weapons.

The Winchester and the Sharps both spoke at once and one man flung up his arms and hurtled out of his saddle. The others started to fan out and before any of them could get a shot in, Zeke squeezed both triggers of the shotgun.

There were howls all around, one man plunged to the ground, and another dropped his sixgun to grasp his useless left arm. The rider furthest away, obviously unhurt, fired at the wagon, the bullet smashing into the woodwork. Moose replied with the carbine and the four remaining horsemen, including the one with the injured arm, wheeled around and fled back up to the tree cover. Like most gun battles, it was all over in seconds, the acrid smoke of gunfire drifting away in the morning air.

Buck pulled the horses to a stop. 'Let's take a look at the two on the ground,' he said. 'Mebbe we'll know the jaspers.'

They walked over to the nearest body, guns cocked and ready for any further attack or any signs of life from the apparent corpses.

Zeke recognised him before they had unmasked the face. 'It's Lem Ritchie. I must say I ain't exactly amazed at him bein' mixed up in this.'

Ritchie had caught most of the shotgun's deadly charge and had died instantly. The other body, shot through the chest, belonged to a stranger.

'One of Ewell's hired hands, I expect,' Moose commented. 'Looks like the game's up for that nest o' rattlers. That one that collected the injured arm, he looked suspiciously like Bull Bartram to me.'

'Yeah,' agreed Buck, 'an' one o' the others was built like a beanpole. I'll lay odds that was Nat Cross.'

'What do we do now?' asked Zeke, peering in the direction the ambushers had gone. 'They've vamoosed over the hill.'

'We go pick 'em up,' Moose said simply. 'We know it's the BE crowd now.'

'Did we ought to wait for the sheriff?' suggested Buck. 'He should be the one to do the arrestin'.'

'By the time he gets back they could have got clean away,' Moose reasoned. 'They know that we know who they are now. They can't bluff it out any more. C'mon, let's load the bodies on to the wagon an' head up to the BE.'

★　★　★

The four remaining bushwhackers, after riding furiously for several miles, slowed down their horses to a trot.

Jim Dawson wiped his grimy, sweating face with his bandanna. 'That didn't work out, what d'we do now?'

At his side, Bull Bartram's face was a

portrayal of bitterness, all of his dreams and hopes shattered. 'I've had enough, we'll never get our hands on that loot now. We'd better get away while we still can.' He grimaced as pain stabbed his shattered arm.

The horseman on his other flank, Bram Ewell, snarled viciously, 'No, we won't. We'll stay an' bluff it out. They can't pin anythin' on us.'

'You do what yuh like, boss,' returned Bartram resignedly. 'I'm headin' back to the ranch for my warbag, then I'm off as far as possible — Wyomin', mebbe.'

Ewell growled, 'An' you others?'

Nat Cross and Dawson looked at each other, then at the foreman and finally at Bram Ewell.

'We're with Bull, Mr. Ewell,' said Cross, nervously. 'We left Lem back there. I've knocked around with him fer many years, now I'll have to make a new start. Besides, when they look at his body, they'll know who we are — they ain't that dumb.'

Ewell was seething. 'Cowards, all of

yuh.' His voice had risen abnormally high, and a twitch had developed in the side of his face.

Some of Bartram's spirit returned. 'No, we ain't cowards, Bram. We're jist seein' things as they are, is all. If'n we stay we'll only finish up in the state penitentiary, or even swingin' on a rope.' He paused and looked at the rancher full in the eyes.

'You promised me a share in a ranch — either yore's or the PF. It was gonna be called the BB. There was a lot of dinero to be found, well, that was it. There's nothin' now. I would have helped yuh — '

'Traitor!' screamed Ewell, his hand diving to his holster. The Colt Navy .36 was out and coming up fast when Bull Bartram finally realised that Ewell intended to shoot him. The foreman's hand had only just reached his gun when the blast hit him full in the chest and he was thrown back in the saddle. Ewell fired two more shots into the falling body, then whirled on the other two.

Nat Cross and Jim Dawson shot their hands in the air, both licking their lips nervously. Ewell's anger seemed to subside and he holstered his pistol.

'Put 'em down, boys, I ain't shootin' yuh. He was greedy. Let's ride to the ranch.'

Callously, he urged his horse on, not looking at the sprawling body on the dusty trail.

They rode in silence to the ranch house, each man busy with his own thoughts. When they arrived, Ewell dismounted and nodded towards the bunkhouse.

'You two get yore things. Then come into the house to collect yore pay. And send Schwarz in if he's there. He can go as well — he's useless to me now.'

He turned his back on the two punchers and strode into the house.

Nat Cross hitched nervously at his pants, which constantly tended to slip whenever he walked, which wasn't very often. 'We'd better be quick, Jim. I don't

228

like the boss in this mood.'

'Yeah,' agreed Dawson, 'he's likely to shoot us in cold blood if'n we put a foot wrong now. If Al's got any sense, he'll come with us, too.'

They walked across to the bunk-house, opened the door and stepped inside. The first thing they saw was Al Schwarz, trussed up like a turkey at Thanksgiving, with a gag in his mouth. Sitting next to him on the floor, in a similar predicament, was the cook.

They heard the door shut behind them, and turned to see Johnny Smith covering them with his thirty-six.

'Mornin', gents,' he said, smiling. 'Been fer a ride with the boss? Where is he, by the way?'

Dawson and Cross raised their hands and looked helplessly around the room. Jim Dawson swallowed hard before he replied.

'He — he's in the house. We jist come for our warbags, then we — '

Johnny was staring hard at the BE puncher. 'Wait a minute — I recognise you. Or rather yore JB. I saw it on the rim of the canyon when yuh ambushed me a coupla weeks back.'

Dawson paled. 'No, not me, yuh didn't. It musta been pore old Bull or one o' the others. Bull wore a similar hat.'

Johnny had not recognised the hat, but thought it worth a try to get some sort of confession out of the puncher. 'What do yuh mean, 'pore old Bull'? What's 'pore' about him?'

'Bram Ewell shot him, not half an hour ago. Dead.'

Johnny's eyebrows went up. 'Why? What did he do?'

Dawson scowled. 'He didn't do nothin'. Jist argued a bit an' told Bram he was gettin' out. Then he shot him.'

Johnny was still standing with his back to the closed door, covering the two cowboys. Suddenly the door was kicked open violently from outside and it caught the youngster full in the back, sending him sprawling to the wooden floor. Bram Ewell stood in the doorway, pistol in his hand.

'I heard that, Jim, an' I don't like what I heard.' Ewell was calm now, ice-cold. 'Mebbe you two hadn't ought to be let loose after all, if'n yo're goin' to spread stories like that around. Keep them hands up,' he added, as both Dawson and Cross started to lower their upraised arms. The offending limbs shot back up.

Ewell turned to the figure of Johnny, now on his hands and knees, his gun having skittered across the floor and under a bunk.

'First I've got to deal with this upstart.'

12

Buck, Zeke and the deputy sat on the wagon and watched the lone rider coming steadily up the trail from town. They had loaded the bodies of Lem and the stranger into the well of the wagon and covered them with the tarp. The weapon that the wounded gunman had discarded proved to be a forty-four Dragoon Colt. 'I'll bet its pardner is still in Bull Bartram's holster,' Moose had remarked drily.

Buck rolled a smoke and lit it. Zeke already had his corncob well alight. Moose peered intently at the oncoming figure. There was something familiar about it, but as yet he could not place the rider. As it was, Zeke's eyesight proved the keenest.

'Thick-set feller, black stetson,' the giant observed between puffs. 'Looks like it might be the sheriff.'

A wave of relief swept over Moose as recognition dawned. 'Thank Gawd fer that. I thought it might be more trouble, but now he can take over.'

Buck grinned. 'I guess yuh ain't cut out to be a lawman, Moose,' he commented.

'I don't mind it when everyone's law-abidin',' replied Moose. 'It's when they git to breakin' it I ain't so keen.'

Hank Rawlins took his time riding up to them. He was obviously a tired man.

'What's up?' he greeted. 'I find the jail empty and you lot out here settin' on a wagon. Where'd the prisoner go, an' what the hell are you all doin' on that wagon?'

Moose told him the story, carefully removing his plainsman hat to show the lump on his head as proof. When he had finished, the sheriff sat in the saddle and carefully rolled a smoke. He said nothing for a full minute while he puffed the quirly into life.

Moose broke the silence. 'Did yuh see Dan's fambly?' he asked.

'Shore, I saw 'em. Took it as well as can be expected.' The sheriff drew heavily on his cigarette. 'But I've been on a kinda double mission. As well as visitin' Houston, I dropped off the train at one point to see a town marshal I used to know, at a little place near El Paso. He showed me a wanted dodger of a man wanted in Texas for murder and cattle rustlin'. The man's name was Barney Everett. The name might have been different, but the picture was that of Bram Ewell. It was him all right.'

'Same initials,' Zeke pointed out. 'Were yuh lookin' fer that kind of evidence especially, Sheriff, or was it jist a hunch? I mean, why Texas?'

'Part hunch, I guess. But I've heard Ewell use the odd Texan expression, an' he's mentioned the state a few times when he's been reminiscin'. But I didn't really expect to come up with somethin' as solid as I've got. I'm on my way now to arrest him, but from what's happened this mornin' it looks like he won't be comin' quietly.'

'He's only got three others with him, an' one of them is hurt bad in the arm or shoulder. Al Schwarz also has a busted hand, his gun hand,' Buck told him. 'We should be able to take 'em without too much bloodshed.'

Hank threw his cigarette down on a patch of stony ground and straightened up in the saddle.

'Come on then, boys, let's go get it over with. I shore appreciate what you boys have done for this town. We won't forget it, you betcha.'

'We ain't quite done yet,' Buck reminded him. 'Save yore thanks till after, Sheriff.'

The sheriff led the way and the wagon trundled along after him, this time Zeke and Moose sitting on top alongside Buck, with the two corpses in the well. They soon joined the main trail to the BE ranch and followed it until they came upon the grisly remains of Bull Bertram, sprawling grotesquely in the middle of the trail.

Hank was first to the body. 'It's

Bartram. He's been shot a number of times. Buckshot in the arm, but that was minor. Revolver bullet in the chest at close range probably killed him, another in his left side, one in the neck. Somebody shore meant it.'

The others joined him on the ground. 'I got him with the shotgun,' said Zeke, looking at the gory mess that had been the BE foreman. 'But nobody else hit him, did yuh, fellers?'

Moose and Buck shook their heads. Neither had even shot at Bartram, and neither had used their sixguns, only the Sharps and the Winchester.

'Well, then,' said the sheriff, 'he was murdered right here on the trail, probably by one of the other gang members. Put him in the wagon with the other bodies. We shore are collectin' 'em today. At this rate there'll be nobody left alive to arrest when we get there.'

Zeke and Moose slung the gruesome carcass into the wagon well, trying unsuccessfully to avoid the mess of

236

blood getting on to their clothes.

'We'd better clean the wagon up before we return it to Mrs. Farrow,' said Buck.

They resumed their journey, more grimly resolved to bring the murderous Ewell to account. A little further along the trail, almost within sight of the ranch house, they rounded a bend and came across two horses and the bewhiskered figure of Repeater Riley. Repeater was examining one of the horses, and turned to face the travellers. He wore an expression of extreme puzzlement on his whiskery, craggy features.

'Ugh, Bull's hoss, Sheriff,' he said without preamble. 'Walkin' home by itself. Bull went out on it. Where's Bull now?' He was so excited that he failed to repeat himself as he blurted the words out.

Hank pointed to the tarpaulin on the wagon. 'He's under there, Repeater. He's dead.'

'Ugh? You killed him, Sheriff?'

'No, I didn't kill him. One of his own crowd did, by the look of it. Thieves fallin' out, I'd say.' Hank gave Repeater a piercing look. 'We're arrestin' all of the BE gang, or what's left of it.'

Repeater blanched. 'What? Me too? Yo're arrestin' me, Sheriff?'

'Depends,' the sheriff replied, 'on what yuh know an' what yuh tell us.'

Repeater's mind was having difficulty grasping all the implications of this blow to his ordered way of life. 'M'job? What about m'job?'

'Yo're job's finished at the BE, I'm afraid, Repeater,' Hank told him. 'Mebbe you'll go to jail, too.'

'No, no, Sheriff. Not jail, please.' He looked appealingly at Moose, Buck and Zeke in turn, hoping they would put in a good word for him.

Buck spoke up. 'Tell us about Lije Guthrie, Repeater. What happened to him?'

Repeater looked anxiously at Buck, started to say something about 'keep m'job' and then grasped that things were a whole lot different now.

'He disappeared. Vanished.'

'Yes, but why?'

Repeater swallowed hard. 'He knew about Pete Farrow, about Pete. He saw it happen. Saw it. Tole me onct.'

'Who was it?' Hank barked. 'Who killed Pete Farrow? Better tell me if'n yuh don't want to go to jail.'

Repeater was scared stiff by now. He hung his head. 'It was Mr. Ewell. That's what Lije tole me. Mr. Ewell.'

Hank's face softened and he clapped a hand on the simpleton's shoulder. 'Yuh jist saved yoreself a jail sentence, Repeater.'

He turned to the others. 'Well, boys, looks like we got all the evidence we need. Let's go roust that hornet's nest.'

The stunning new events had driven all thoughts of telling the sheriff about Johnny's visit to the ranch from Repeater's mind, if, indeed, he would ever have remembered.

'It's all yore fault, damn yuh,' Bram Ewell told Johnny, who had been ordered to remain on the floor, now seated with his hands on his head. Ewell's pistol wavered between Johnny and the two BE punchers, standing with raised arms.

'Yuh sent for yore pa, an' he hired those two interfering detectives, or whatever they claim to be.' Ewell's eyes were blazing in an evil fashion. 'Everythin' was goin' well, Alice was goin' to marry me, an' even if she didn't I would have got her ranch an' found the money. I knew it was there, hidden away some place.'

Ewell's gun stopped its wavering and the nozzle pointed directly at the helpless Johnny. 'So for that, I'm gonna kill yuh. Now. I shoulda told the boys to finish you off when they had yuh holed up in the cave.'

Nat Cross blurted out, 'But, Boss, don'tcha think there's been enough — '

'Shut up!' snarled Ewell.

Scared as he was, Cross persisted. 'The depitty an' those other two know who we are now, Bram. They'll be here any minute. Didn't we ought — '

Ewell barked a short, scornful laugh. 'I know Moose, he'll wait for the sheriff comin' back, I betcha. By then we'll be long gone.'

As he turned back to Johnny, a window shattered, showering glass into the room. Moose's Sharps poked through. Ewell immediately fired at the window and heard a gasp. Hank's voice came from behind the door. 'Drop yore weapons in there. This is the law.'

Ewell turned and fired at the door. Cross and Dawson dived to join Johnny on the floor. A number of things happened then in the space of a few seconds. As Ewell's attention was distracted, Johnny reached for his gun under the bunk. A window on the other side of the bunkhouse was flung open and Buck leaped in the room, Colt drawn. Hank kicked the door open as the rancher whirled to face Buck. But it was the Sharps which blasted, filling the room with acrid smoke.

As the gunsmoke slowly drifted out of

the windows, they could see Ewell lying in a pool of blood, the side of his head torn away by the carbine slug. A number of guns covered Cross and Dawson, but they offered no resistance. Hank called to Moose, who was still outside.

'You all right, Moose? Did he hit yuh?'

'Dad-blasted shoulder, is all,' came the reply. 'But I reckon I paid him back, an' good.'

'Yuh shore did,' answered Buck, looking at the body on the floor.

'How about me?' asked Johnny. 'Am I still under arrest?'

'I guess that's up to Moose, Johnny.' Buck grinned, his eyes twinkling. 'He was pretty sore about that crack on the haid yuh gave him. Mebbe he'll let yuh off with ten years.'

★   ★   ★

There was a lot of activity in the Peaceful area for the next few days. The coroner pronounced the bandits as dying from gunshot wounds, the bodies were buried and the cases of Dan Beardow and Pete Farrow closed. After Johnny and Frank Smith had had a joyful reunion, they went their separate ways, Johnny visiting the Langham spread a lot, and Frank spending quite some time at the PF ranch.

Sheriff Hank Rawlins suggested to his deputy that since Johnny had voluntarily entered the jail he was entitled to leave whenever he felt like it, especially as he was innocent of the charge. Moose, who had grown more tolerant as the lump on his head subsided did, however, think that some payment should be made for an assault on a peace officer, so they agreed on a fine of ten dollars, which Johnny's father gladly paid.

Buck and Zeke hung around, spending some of the fifty dollars each they received from Frank Smith as a bonus for completing the case. Most of it was spent in Ed Williamson's emporium, so they were the first to hear that Ed had a case of 'sump'n special' in and would be releasing it on his unsuspecting customers next Saturday night. Everyone was invited, a kind of celebration for the return of peace to Peaceful.

Needless to say, the Bald Eagle was packed to suffocation on Saturday night, all the townsfolk and all the ranchers being well represented. But it was Luke Simms who was first to broach the subject of Ed's special treat.

'Yuh said yuh'd got sump'n special, Ed,' the little stage-driver reminded him. 'What is it?'

Ed grinned. 'I guess you boys ain't never had any real Scotch, have yuh?' He bent down behind the counter and produced a case of the amber nectar.

'I have,' admitted Frank Smith, 'it's quite easy to obtain in Boston.'

'Yo're a different kettle of fish to this rabble, Mr. Smith,' said Ed, taking a bottle out of the case. 'Here, try it, you heathens.'

Luke read the label suspiciously.

'Hey, lookit that. They can't even spell it properly.' He pointed to the word 'whisky'. 'They missed the 'e' out of whiskey.' He snorted disgustedly.

'That's how they spell it in Scotland,' explained Ed patiently. 'Why don't yuh try drinkin' it, not readin' it?'

They all sampled the Scotch and pronounced it excellent.

'Well,' admitted Luke, 'mebbe they can't spell over there, but they shore can brew whisky.'

'Hey, Johnny,' said Duke Summerville, peering through the blue haze of smoke from assorted cigarettes, pipes and cigars. 'Watcha gonna do now? Mebbe Bill Langham will take yuh on, specially now yo're courtin' Kate.'

Frank Smith spared his son's blushes. 'You'll come and be our foreman, won't you, Johnny? Mine and Alice's.'

'Hey, no kiddin', Dad. Yuh asked her to marry yuh?'

'And she accepted, son. So I'll be staying out here and keeping an eye on you.'

'How about a double weddin', you two?' suggested Buck.

'That's a mighty fine idea,' said Johnny. 'I'll suggest it tomorrow to Kate.'

A tall, imposing looking man, wearing the badge of a U.S. Marshal, shouldered his way up to the bar.

'I'm lookin' for the sheriff,' he told Ed. 'Is he in here, the rest of the town seems deserted?'

'Yeah, I'm here, Marshal,' Hank announced, pushing through the crowd. 'What can I do for yuh?'

'I'm here to take yore prisoner to the county seat, Sheriff.'

'Oh, hell,' gasped the sheriff, 'I plumb forgot to send a wire in all the excitement. I meant to cancel yore visit.'

'Yuh mean there's no charge? No crime has been committed?'

'There was a crime, all right. Jist a case of right crime, wrong man.'

Other tides in the
Linford Western Library

THE CROOKED SHERIFF
John Dyson

Black Pete Bowen quit Texas with a burning hatred of men who try to take the law into their own hands. But he discovers that things aren't much different in the silver mountains of Arizona.

THEY'LL HANG BILLY FOR SURE: LARRY & STRETCH
Marshall Grover

Billy Reese, the West's most notorious desperado, was to stand trial. From all compass points came the curious and the greedy, the riff-raff of the frontier. Suddenly, a crazed killer was on the loose — but the Texas Trouble-Shooters were there, girding their loins for action.

RIDERS OF RIFLE RANGE
Wade Hamilton

Veterinarian Jeff Jones did not like open warfare — but it was there on Scrub Pine grass. When he diagnosed a sick bull on the Endicott ranch as having the contagious blackleg disease, he got involved in the warfare — whether he liked it or not!

THE WEST WITCH
Lance Howard

Detective Quinton Hilcrest journeys west, seeking the Black Hood Bandits' lost fortune. Within hours of arriving in Hags Bend, he is fighting for his life, ensnared with a beautiful outcast the town claims is a witch! Can he save the young woman from the angry mob?

BLACK JO OF THE PECOS
Jeff Blaine

Nobody knew where Black Josephine Callard came from or whither she returned. Deputy U.S. Marshal Frank Haggard would have to exercise all his cunning and ability to stay alive before he could defeat her highly successful gang and solve the mystery.

RIDE FOR YOUR LIFE
Johnny Mack Bride

They rode west, hoping for a new start. Then they met another broken-down casualty of war, and he had a plan that might deliver them from despair. But the only men who would attempt it would be the truly brave — or the desperate. They were both.

THE NIGHTHAWK
Charles Burnham

While John Baxter sat looking at the ruin that arsonists had made of his log house, a stranger rode into the yard. Baxter and Walt Showalter partnered up and re-built the house. But when it was dynamited, they struck back — and all hell broke loose.

BEAR PAW
Nevada Carter

Austin Dailey traded two cows to a pair of Indians for a bay horse, which subsequently disappeared. Tracks led to a secret hideout of fugitive Indians — and cattle thieves. Indians and stockmen co-operated against the rustlers. But it was Pale Woman who acted as interpreter between her people and the rangemen.